A CUP FULL OF POISON

Isabella Bassett

Copyright © 2025 Isabella Bassett

All rights reserved

This is a work of fiction. Names, characters, places, and incidents either are the product of the author's imagination or are used fictitiously. Any similarity to real persons, living or dead, is coincidental and not intended by the author.

No part of this book may be reproduced, or stored in a retrieval system, or transmitted in any form or by any means, electronic, mechanical, photocopying, recording, or otherwise, without express written permission of the publisher.

CONTENTS

Title Page
Copyright
Chapter 1   1
Chapter 2   10
Chapter 3   20
Chapter 4   30
Chapter 5   39
Chapter 6   49
Chapter 7   59
Chapter 8   69
Chapter 9   80
Chapter 10   90
Chapter 11   100
Chapter 12   112
Chapter 13   122
Chapter 14   132
Chapter 15   143

Chapter 16	154
Chapter 17	165
Chapter 18	176
Chapter 19	187
Chapter 20	198
Chapter 21	209
Chapter 22	220
Chapter 23	233
Books by Isabella Bassett	249

CHAPTER 1

Summer 1926

"Death," Aunt Mable whispered from a corner in the room. The murmur was low enough to suggest a desire for concealment, but in the hush of the drawing room the pronouncement carried.

Since this was the fourth time she had drawn the ominous card this morning, however, no one paid it much heed. Only her two sisters, my aunts Mavis and Myrtle, still seemed to ascribe any significance to its recurrence. Each time the card sprang forth, they scrambled to stuff it back into the Tarot deck and then promptly reshuffled it with the wide-eyed look of serfs playing Russian roulette with their master's revolver. But their effort at hiding the card was thwarted each time. Death, it would seem, would not be ignored.

"I hope it's not the Vicar," said Aunt Mavis, looking up from her place at the cards table. Her sisters followed her gaze towards the tall windows overlooking the gardens.

Just at that moment, the Vicar was streaking

past, shrieking, a swarm of bees in pursuit. It was owing to the bees that we were currently confined to the relative safety of the indoors.

Two weeks remained until my brother Edward's wedding, and the household was in a flutter. With hordes of relatives and guests expected to begin arriving in the next few days, bedrooms not used since William III had visited for a fortnight in 1689, on his way to the Battle of Walcourt, had to be refreshed. Though the house was always beautiful, Mother would leave nothing to chance, or to Aunt Ida's scrutiny. Servants were dusting, mopping, beating rugs, polishing brass, and cleaning silver. Every available ladder in the neighborhood was now propped up against a wall somewhere in the castle, and every boy and girl old enough to hold a feather duster was to be found at the top of said ladder stabbing at the cobwebs.

"It's harvest time, my dear," Father had tried to reason with Mother. "The tenants need their children in the fields."

Mother had waved his scruples away. Though the daughter of an American industrialist, she had taken to the role of a feudal ruler, upon marriage to Father, the Earl of Beasley, with aplomb. "I just know your Aunt Ida will use her stay here as an invitation to run a finger over the embrasures in the darkest tower," Mother had countered. It was an objection Father could not refute.

As part of this general state of frenzy, the

workmen tasked with erecting the large marquee Mother had ordered had insisted on a trial run this morning. They'd had their doubts the contrivance would fit in the space designated for it in the gardens. It hadn't. In the process, an inopportune gust of wind had turned the unsecured marquee into something resembling the sail of a longboat. The tent had shot right through the lawn and into Father's bee sanctuary, wiping out beehives in its course.

The bees had not taken kindly to this Viking-like raid.

To help him corral the runagates, Father had called upon the Vicar, a fellow bee enthusiast. It soon transpired, however, that while the Vicar adored bees, and liked to identify with Saint Ambrose in his affinity for these usually docile creatures, Father's bees did not return the sentiment. As the bees descended upon the Vicar with the fervor of Anglo-Saxons defending their farms, and as he dashed across the lawn, one began to suspect that Father's insistence on summoning the Vicar had been an underhanded plan to draw the bees away from the workmen.

"I wouldn't worry about it, dear," Aunt Myrtle called to Mother, pulling my attention away from the spectacle in the gardens. Whether she meant the Vicar or the Death card was not clear, but her voice held little conviction.

In reply, Mother simply smiled gracefully from

her spot on the sofa, remaining unmoved by the prophesying of the cards. She rarely attended to the divinations of Father's sisters.

Still, I could tell something was preoccupying Mother. Were she a woman to display agitation, Mother might have tapped her elegant foot or drummed her slender fingers. As it was, the only indication that anything was amiss lay in her discreet peeks at the carriage clock upon the mantelpiece.

Perhaps mistaking these glances for an acknowledgment of the inevitable, Aunt Myrtle felt called upon to add, "It's an auspicious sign, dear." The look she shared with her sisters, however, suggested that such an optimistic outcome had long ceased to be an option.

To their credit, in the wake of this half-hearted reassurance by Aunt Myrtle—whatever doubts they held inwardly—the other two sisters rushed to placate Mother. As they had done each time previously, they vowed the Death card meant nothing more sinister than "new beginnings" and "good tidings". But their effusions had grown less sincere with each reiteration, and now they kept casting uneasy looks at the door, as though expecting Death itself to walk in.

So it was with something of a jump that they received the hurried entrance of the butler.

"A telegram, my lady," Cuthbert said as he stepped towards Mother and presented her with a note on a silver salver. She grabbed it with uncharacteristic haste.

As the days to the wedding had fallen away, telegrams from relatives with various excuses, requests, demands, and grievances had begun to pile up. The telegrams usually followed the format of recounting some weighty grievance about a relative, demanding not to be placed in a bedroom too near them, and then proceeding to offhandedly request the accommodation of some outlandish dietary requirement during their stay, invoking a recommendation by their doctor as an excuse.

Mother regarded the dispatch address on the envelope with growing distaste. "What pretext has the old devil cooked up this time?" she said. "I know quite well the Worcestershire Flower Show is at the end of this week."

I tried to hide my smile. The mention of the flower show could only mean that the missive was from Uncle Albert.

It had been news from Uncle that Mother had been expecting all morning. He was supposed to have departed an hour ago, with strict instructions to his household to telephone once he was safely on his way. No such communication had come through. A telegram, however, was a rather dramatic way of communicating his departure.

"Your uncle will do anything to attend the

flower show prior to coming here," Mother added, sparing me an accusatory glance that suggested I was somehow responsible for Uncle.

I felt it was rather unfair to be reprimanded for Uncle's failings just because I was his Private Secretary—and not a very diligent one at that—but I appreciated Mother's point. He had avoided coming to our house for over a week now, each time presenting us with a wilder story of what precluded his departure—fires, break-ins, thefts. I conceded that Mother had cause to worry that, once again, Uncle had found a pretext to avoid making a start.

One could say that Mother had brought this upon herself. She had insisted that the more calamity-prone relatives, such as Uncle Albert and Father's sisters, were to arrive early for the wedding. "That way, the old dears can settle in before the rest of the guests arrive," she had said. What she'd meant was that she wanted to keep them under her command and hopefully minimize their predilection for getting into trouble. Father's sisters had obeyed the summons, perhaps lured by the promise of a steady fire in the grate and three hot meals a day, but Uncle Albert had proved more crafty at avoiding this trap.

Mother opened the telegram, and as I watched her read it, I could see her expression change. Her beautifully drawn eyebrows gathered in a frown. "What on Earth could he mean?!"

Cuthbert, who had been heading out of the room, halted upon her exclamation, suddenly quite taken with a speck of dust on the table by the door. I knew the household staff had an ongoing wager as to what reason Uncle Albert would come up with next to avoid coming under Mother's reign too early. We all knew that he wasn't going to miss Edward's wedding, but he was not too keen to spend more time with Mother than was strictly necessary. Between Mother, who was forever making demands on his hobbies, or making comments about the propriety of his behavior, and the impending arrival of Aunt Ida, his nemesis, who was forever needling him about the deficiencies of his butterfly collection, I could see why Uncle Albert was not too eager to get here fast.

As intrigued as Cuthbert, but with more agency to satisfy my curiosity, I reached for the telegram. Mother handed it to me without resistance. This amenable gesture, a touch uncharacteristic of her, aroused suspicion in me, and I looked down at the paper with interest. "Departure postponed," I read aloud, as much for my benefit as Cuthbert's. "A body in the library." I looked up at Mother, perplexed, but her countenance conveyed exasperation rather than surprise or worry.

Before I could assimilate the meaning behind the words, however, my aunts materialized by my side. Aunt Mable snatched at the telegram with ill-concealed glee. "A body in the library!" she repeated, as though making certain I had read it correctly. The sisters huddled together, each glaring at the slip of paper in turn, making approving sounds. It put one in mind of the Graeae from Greek mythology, passing around their one eye for a better look at Perseus.

"It's rather satisfying when one's proclamations come to pass," Aunt Mavis said, her sisters nodding in assent.

I wanted to remind them that not a minute before, they had argued that the Death card was the most fortuitous card in the Tarot deck. But it was perhaps wiser to remain silent on that point.

Despite appearances, my aunts Mable, Mavis and Myrtle were gentle creatures. One could not blame them for occasionally lapsing into schadenfreude. Life had been unkind to them. It had saddled them with unscrupulous husbands who had deprived them of their fortunes. Perhaps in gratitude to Fate, who had eventually intervened to rid them of the scoundrels—though not soon enough, thus leaving the sisters destitute in their old age—my aunts now devoted their time to divining the future. Their fondness for the occult perhaps also helped explain why they looked the part of carnival fortunetellers, with clothes in different states of disarray, dripping in shawls, beads and lace. Their sole concession to the noble class into which they were born was the taut little bun each wore to contain her gray hair.

"What does Uncle Albert mean by all this?!" Mother asked again, this time with irritation.

Before anyone could hazard a guess, however, Father came in, making Cuthbert jump out of the way of the swinging door.

CHAPTER 2

Father bore all the signs of his latest hobby: an apron smeared liberally with honey, a few dead bees tangled in his hair, and an entourage of dogs with wagging tails licking the trail of sticky footprints left in his wake. While Father had been stung more times than he cared to admit, thus far he'd only had a thimbleful of honey to show for his efforts. This lack of success did not diminish the joy he found in the activity, perchance because Mother was rather weary of the winged creatures.

"I saw the telegram boy running up the lane," Father said, slightly out of breath, as though he himself had come running. "Is it a relative?!"

To the casual observer, Father's question, given the nature of Uncle Albert's telegram, might sound surprisingly prescient. One might wonder if he happened to possess the very powers of clairvoyance so coveted by his sisters.

Nothing, however, could be further from the truth.

His remark stemmed from a rather more

prosaic source—namely, his eagerness that the forthcoming wedding might somehow be derailed. Father would never admit it aloud, but he was longing for some sort of catastrophe to postpone the wedding, not because he didn't want to see my brother married, but because he dreaded giving a speech in front of all the guests. Especially Aunt Ida.

In the early days of their visit, Father had ardently encouraged his sisters to ask the Spirits if perhaps some calamity might not befall Aunt Ida. The Spirits, however, had appeared rather reluctant to commit to such an assurance. I quite understood their timidity. After all, one suspected Aunt Ida of being quite a dab hand at manipulating the Dark Forces. It would not do to cross her.

Now, as the fateful day drew closer, Father hoped, rather uncharitably, that a telegram might arrive from a sinking ship carrying the American relations across the Atlantic. Nothing too deadly, of course...sufficient lifeboats on board, and such. He simply hoped for some modest divine intervention to prevent him from wearing the morning suit Mother had selected for him, and furthermore—and perhaps more pressingly—from having to deliver his speech.

It was this fear of public speaking that had chiefly held back Father from the illustrious political career Mother had imagined for him. Now, it made him wish for a delay in the wedding.

Fear made people wish for silly things.

"It's a body in Bertie's library!" Aunt Myrtle cried.

"I say!" Father said and jumped to his sister's side to assess the telegram's likelihood of getting him out of the wedding's forced declamation.

"This is precisely why I wanted Uncle Albert here early," Mother said. "I daresay this is one of his less brilliant ideas to evade a family obligation."

"I doubt even Bertie would invent a body just to avoid driving down today," Father said gently. His visage, however, suggested that he wished he'd had the temerity to invent such a story himself.

Mother gave him a withering look. "A dead body is just about the *only* thing Uncle Albert has not tried," she countered.

"But who can it be?" I asked, though no one seemed to hear me.

"It's bound to bring the Press," Mother continued, betraying her priorities. "Of course one wants them here for the wedding, but not under such circumstances."

She sighed.

Sometimes, I felt sorry for Mother. Beautiful and confident, she ruled with steely glances. And while the house and her social calendar ran like clockwork, and she had cowered or charmed —as the person's social standing permitted—all acquaintances into submission, she had never quite managed to subdue the family. Around every corner lurked a family member trying to thwart her success. Between the follies of Uncle Albert, Father's sisters, Father, and, indeed, sometimes even me, I wondered at Mother's continued resolve to strive for perfection.

A tinge of pity pricked in my stomach for her as I took in the scene in the drawing room. The Aunts were hunched over the telegram like witches cackling over a cauldron, Father was dripping honey while the occasional bee buzzed in his hair, and the dogs were rolling around, rubbing their sticky backs on the Aubusson rug. The wedding was shaping up to be another trying family occasion for Mother.

As though sensing my compassion, Mother stood up and plucked the telegram out of Aunt Mable's hand. "Well, the Spirits have had their pound of flesh—"

"Indeed! They'll be thrilled to hear the message got through," Aunt Mable said, missing Mother's sarcasm.

"But what are we to do about Uncle Albert?" Mother continued, exasperated.

Still feeling well-disposed towards Mother, I rushed to the telephone before the sentiment passed, to make inquiries as to the veracity of the telegram.

"I say, Wilford," I addressed Uncle's trusty valet down the telephone line, once we were connected, "this would not be one of Uncle's feeble attempts to delay his departure, would it? Mother is quite aware he'd like to attend the upcoming flower show," I continued, trying out her idea. Though I would never say it in front of Mother, it was just the type of scheme Uncle Albert would concoct to slink out of a responsibility.

"I assure you, my lady," Wilford said stoically from the other end of the line, "that though the message does bear all the hallmarks of a scheme Lord Tatham would invent, and although he is very keen on being personally present at the Worcestershire Flower Show, on this occasion I fear that the contents of the message are quite genuine."

I gasped. "In that case, it's quite concerning!"

"Indeed, my lady."

"And who is it?"

"The Hon. Major Richard Yardley," Wilford said in a tone that suggested I should be familiar with the chap.

The name was rather pompous, and something about it sounded vaguely familiar. I wondered where I had heard it before, but it was a matter I could inquire into later.

"Have the police been called?" I asked instead.

"The police?" Wilford sounded a bit taken aback. "No, my lady. According to the doctor, the death was quite natural. A heart attack."

Though Wilford relayed this information in a monotonous voice, as though Majors made a habit of dropping dead in Uncle's library as a matter of course, the entire thing seemed rather extraordinary to me. Who was this Major? And what was he doing dying in Uncle's library?

"But if I may add," Wilford continued, interrupting my thoughts, "your uncle is most anxious for your assistance in a related matter. He's requested that I instruct you to drive down to the estate today."

"He's not in any trouble, is he?" I asked. It would be just like Uncle to make himself suspicious to the police even in a case of natural death.

"Not as such, my lady," Wilford said. "But perhaps the details are best not discussed over the telephone," he said pointedly. "His Lordship is adamant that any communication at a distance pertaining to his, er, problem be conducted over telegrams."

Yes, telephones were notoriously leaky. One knew that even though operators were not allowed to listen in on conversations, they were always the first to know the latest gossip. And though my uncle placed a Victorian sense of sanctity upon telegrams, they were, of course, read by the postal clerks who dispatched them.

"Lord Tatham insists on your earliest departure," Wilford implored down the line.

"I'll see what I can do," I said with more confidence than I felt. Mother was unlikely to let me go, my employment as Uncle's secretary notwithstanding.

Truth was, I would not have minded the diversion. Like Father, I was not much looking forward to the wedding, and found little enjoyment in the preparations. As I was still unmarried, Mother had a tendency to ruin any social gathering for me with her machinations. I had spied the seating chart for the wedding reception and ascertained that it would be just such an occasion. I was sitting at a table between Cecil, Lady Morton's son, and Gabriel, Lady Ansley's son, both unattractive prospects. James, my chosen beau, was seated at a faraway table with all the vivacious debutantes.

As I walked back to the drawing room, I wondered what excuse I could use to make my way to Uncle Albert's place. The likelihood of Mother acquiescing to Uncle's request was minimal. She was trying to corral us, not have us running around the countryside.

"What news?" Mother said as I entered the drawing room. I noticed that Father and his dogs were gone. Perhaps he'd succumbed to the Vicar's moving pleas for help wafting in from the outside.

"It is indeed a body, I'm afraid," I said. "The Hon. Major Richard Yardley was found in Uncle's library. Apparently he'd suffered a heart attack."

"Major Yardley?!" Mother cried.

"How exciting!" Aunt Mable exclaimed at the same time, her voice colored with rather unbecoming delight in the circumstances. I hoped she was referring to the uncanny coincidence of the cards' manifestation rather than the Major's death.

"Do you know him?" I said, turning to Mother. "The name did sound familiar, but I could not place it."

"I'm surprised, Caroline," she said, casting me a disapproving glance. "Yardley is your uncle's family name. Before he came into his title, he was Albert Yardley, with the courtesy title of Viscount Cartwhile."

Of course, that's where I'd heard the name. While I'd only ever really known Uncle Albert after he'd come into his title, I must have heard his family name at some point. The possibility of a familial connection between the dead Major and Uncle was quite tantalizing. Surely, the Major's presence in Uncle's library could not be accidental, I mused, intrigued.

"So Major Yardley is some sort of relation?" I pressed for more information. But the Major's name seemed to have caused a bit of commotion in the drawing room, and no one paid me any attention.

The aunts had by now surrounded Mother on the sofa, much to her distress. I sat down in a chair facing them.

"They could not have seen each other since Richard was a young child," said Aunt Mavis.

"He and Bertie never got on," added Aunt Mable.

"And who doesn't get on with Bertie?" reasoned Aunt Myrtle.

"Richard was a bad lot," said Aunt Mavis rather forcefully.

Aunt Myrtle gasped. "Do not speak ill of the dead, sister! He was troubled, perhaps," she amended.

Aunt Mable leaned forward conspiratorially. "There was a girl involved," she whispered in Victorian outrage.

"Isn't that always the case with troublesome young men?" said Aunt Mavis

"Something tragic happened to her," added Aunt Mable.

"Oh, but that was after he'd left," objected Aunt Myrtle.

The sisters proceeded to speak over each other, as was their habit, each trying to outdo the next.

"And yet, they say he left the village in a hurry—"

"He went out to India—"

"Joined the Army—"

"Did well for himself…a Major," Aunt Mavis said, almost regretfully.

"Well, now," interjected Aunt Mable, "I don't know if one could call that an achievement. After twenty years in the Army, and as the son of an earl, he should have made Colonel by now."

"Yes, but who is he?!" I cried, tired of the deluge of unanchored gossip.

"Why, don't you know?!" Aunt Mable said, looking at me as though seeing me for the first time today.

Mother raised a hand to forestall the Aunts and sighed. Her voice, when it came out, was rather somber. "He's your Uncle Albert's brother."

CHAPTER 3

"Brother?!" I cried, astonished. It was a good thing I was sitting down. I had never heard anything so unexpected. "Uncle Albert had a brother!"

How could that be?! I searched my thoughts for a reasonable explanation. Many years separated Uncle Albert and me, and I had never paid much attention to his life prior to becoming his secretary, a little over a year ago. And granted, Uncle Albert was quite a distant relation. As Father's second cousin once removed, the title of *Uncle* was bestowed upon him out of courtesy rather than anything else. But still! How had the matter of Uncle Albert's having a brother never been discussed, either by my family or by him?

I turned to my mother, awaiting clarification.

"Major Richard Yardley is—or rather, was—a son from Uncle Albert's father's second marriage," Mother said. "Our connection to Uncle Albert is through his mother, who was the daughter of your father's great-grandmother's brother. The late Lord Tatham's second family is no blood relation of ours. Our families were never acquainted, as we have never moved in the same circles."

My mind tried to keep up with the logic of relations—albeit step-relations—being so easily dismissed. Why did I not know any of this?

"I believe there was some unpleasantness about the second wife and the children," Aunt Mable said.

"Children!?" I cried. How many of these secret half-siblings were there?

"I would not go as far as that," Aunt Myrtle chastised her sister, ignoring my outburst. "She was simply not brought up very highly. A pretty thing, but with no social standing."

"A morganatic marriage," Aunt Mavis whispered.

"Are we allowed to say that nowadays?" Aunt Myrtle asked, her voice tinged with mild alarm.

"How many more step-siblings does Uncle Albert have?" I was more insistent this time.

"There were three sons from the second marriage," Mother said. And though the tone in which she delivered this morsel suggested the topic was disagreeable to her, the manner in which she followed my aunts' every word made it plain that most of this was news to her as well.

"And why have I never met these brothers?" I inquired. Why had Uncle's half-brothers never been invited to family gatherings? Or even mentioned?

Aunt Mable turned to me. "Your Uncle Albert's mother was a lady, with a title and money of her own. The mother of his step-brothers was a nobody. One could not associate with them socially, you see."

"The title of Lord Tatham, of course, went to your uncle, as did the estate," Aunt Mavis added.

Aha! The question of title. That, more than anything else, perhaps explained why Uncle was well-received in the family, but I'd never heard of his poor relations.

"But they had the same father," I objected.

"The only thing their birth was good for was to establish them in respectable professions," said Aunt Mavis. "The Army, the Church, the Law."

"All as is expected from the untitled sons of a peer of the realm," Aunt Mable concurred.

I flinched at the harshness of their words, but it was the uncompromising reality of titled families. James, as the fourth son of an earl, had to make his own way in the world. His lack of funds and inability to support a family was one of the reasons we had not made our engagement official.

Aunt Mavis cut into my thoughts. "Richard, the oldest, went into the Indian Army—"

Her sisters took up the challenge and plunged into a race of sorts.

"Bernard, into the Church—"

"And Eliot, the youngest, studied law—"

"With the estate tied to the title, there was really no money for any of them—"

"I believe Bertie did quite a lot to help them when their father passed away—"

"Their father died quite soon after Richard left for India. Within a year, I would say—"

"Richard was something of a favorite—"

"Handsome—"

"Yes, but Bertie was the firstborn. Nothing can overthrow primogeniture—"

"Richard's abrupt departure probably did their father in—"

"The father was quite old by then," Aunt Myrtle offered in a reassuring tone.

The sisters paused for a collective breath. But instead of proceeding, each appeared momentarily lost in thought.

My mind was racing with all I'd learned. I hardly knew where to begin with my questions. Instead, I simply stared from one aunt to the next, wondering how they knew so much about Uncle Albert's step-family. My aunts were closer in age to Uncle Albert than to Father, who had been the baby of the family—the long-awaited son and heir. His sisters must have known Uncle Albert well in his youth, and by extension, his family drama too.

It was Aunt Mable who first resumed speaking. "I don't believe your Uncle Albert has seen his brother since Richard was a young boy."

"When his father remarried, your Uncle Albert took on various government posts across the Empire, returning to England only occasionally," added Aunt Mavis.

"Probably didn't wish to be in the way of his father's new family," Aunt Myrtle elucidated. "Bertie is such a sensitive soul."

"By the time Bertie settled permanently back in England, upon the death of their father," said Aunt Mavis, "Richard was already in India."

"And he never came back to England again," Aunt Mable elaborated.

"Until now, it would seem," added Aunt Mavis.

"That would make it close to twenty-five years," said Aunt Myrtle thoughtfully.

"Why did he stay away for so long?" I asked, my curiosity aroused by this anomaly.

"The details were never discussed," said Aunt Mable, "but it probably stemmed from the disagreement between him and his father."

"About the young woman?" I ventured.

Aunt Mavis nodded.

"Most unsuitable, it was said," Aunt Myrtle delivered in a hushed tone.

"His father greatly disapproved of Richard's interest in her—"

"Like father, like son, seduced by a pretty face rather than class—"

"Yes, the father himself was a scoundrel.

Choosing for his second wife a young woman with no social connections. And at his age, and so late in life—"

"But she died before him, leaving the three boys, aged no more than ten or twelve, in the care of that old curmudgeon—"

"No wonder Richard ran away the first chance he got—"

"Rebelled under his father's tyranny—"

"Yes, Bertie's father was not a pleasant man. It's rather surprising that Bertie is such a well-adjusted man—"

I glanced at Aunt Myrtle, who had supplied that nugget, with suspicion. I did not share her assessment of Uncle Albert.

"How old was Richard when he left?" I asked.

"About twenty," Aunt Mavis said.

"What happened to the girl?" I asked.

"Which girl?" Aunt Mavis parried.

"The one he'd quarreled with his father over," I said, trying to keep my exasperation in check.

"Oh, as that was nothing to do with Bertie, I can't really recall the details," Aunt Mavis replied.

I looked at the others in hope, but they merely nodded in agreement.

"Something tragic," supplied Aunt Myrtle rather unhelpfully.

We had reached an impasse.

"I wonder what brought Richard back?" Aunt

Mable said after a few moments, echoing my own thoughts.

"And what was he doing in Bertie's library, of all places?" added Aunt Mavis.

"They were not on the best of terms," elaborated Aunt Myrtle.

"Yes, there was always some resentment between the two," said Aunt Mable.

"Perhaps Richard felt cheated. As the oldest of the sons from the second marriage, all that stood between him and the peerage was Uncle Albert," added Aunt Mavis.

"I wonder why Richard never did anything about it?" Aunt Mable mused.

"Oh, how wicked of you to say that," admonished Aunt Mavis, though one could see that the idea was not entirely distasteful to her.

The notion seemed to amuse my aunts. They paused for a moment before rushing to expound on that theory.

"Perhaps that's precisely why Richard came back—"

"Bertie has had a rather long life—"

"And has cheated death more than once—"

"Perhaps Richard came to hasten his departure—"

I cast a weary glance at Aunt Mable upon that suggestion.

"Perhaps Bertie did something about it,"

countered Aunt Mavis.

"Are you suggesting Uncle Albert killed his brother?" I asked, incredulous.

"In self-defense only, of course," she hedged.

"Surely it would not be within Uncle's capacity to kill an Army man, especially one twenty years his junior," I objected. Thinking of Uncle's stooped body, arthritic hands, fluffy white hair, dressed in smoking jacket and fez, I could hardly picture him attacking anyone.

"Oh, Bertie doesn't need physical strength to topple a grown man," said Aunt Myrtle quietly.

"There are much cleverer—"

"And subtler—" put in Aunt Mavis.

"—ways to bring down a grown man," Aunt Mable concluded.

"Why are we even discussing this?" I asked, startled by the turn the conversation had taken. "The local doctor has concluded that the Major died of a heart attack."

The aunts nodded with a knowing glint in their eyes.

"There are plenty of poisonous plants—oleander, foxglove, lily of the valley, yew, monkshood—that mimic heart attacks," said Aunt Mable, counting the names off on her fingers.

"Poisonous plants have never been in short supply in your uncle's garden," Aunt Mavis said.

I studied the frail women. How did they know

so much about poisons? I had long suspected that at least one of my aunts had done away with her ne'er-do-well husband. Perhaps they were not as defenseless as I had assumed.

"One wonders that there haven't been more accidental deaths on that estate," Mother added dryly.

I turned to look at Mother. She appeared to have grown pale at all this talk of Uncle Albert poisoning his half-brother. Surely she didn't believe my aunts' wild conjectures. People dying of natural causes was quite... natural. So what was troubling her?

"What is it?" I asked Mother.

"The Press are sure to love this," she said, waving a hand towards my aunts, as though to illustrate all the excitement the Major's death would elicit.

"Surely the Major's demise can have no bearing on us, or the wedding. He's a distant relation, and his death was of natural causes," I said, trying to reassure her.

"Yes, but reporters are sure to make the most of it," Mother countered, her tone anxious. "A half-brother dying in the library of a peer of the realm—and a member of the Lords, no less. Your uncle is bound to make a fool of himself one way or another."

Uncle hardly needed a dead body in his library to do that, I quipped internally. While Mother would have agreed with this witticism, I refrained from sharing it with her. The way her eyes flicked restlessly around the room, I could tell she was busy hatching a plan.

She turned to me suddenly. "It's imperative that you bring your Uncle Albert here at once," she said. "If he had left a few days ago, as I'd instructed him, we would not be in this situation."

Mother's argument was not entirely logical—the Major would have been likely to die regardless of where Uncle was billeted—but I did not object. Instead, I seized my chance, and was out of the drawing room and on the road within the hour.

CHAPTER 4

Driving to Worcestershire, I tried to review all I had learned from my aunts. Uncle Albert's father had married a second, much younger woman of inferior social standing. Uncle Albert, then in his mid-twenties, had left England soon after his father's remarriage and had lived across the Empire. When his father's second wife had died, the three boys from the marriage, still quite young, were left in the care of their father, who was by then old and of a rather difficult disposition.

For a moment I wondered about Uncle's other two step-brothers. What had happened to them? Where were they now? My aunts had only mentioned that one had become a parson and the other a barrister. As Uncle had never mentioned them to me, he could not have a very close relationship with them, I concluded.

I resumed my exploration of Richard's life. Several things had happened in quick succession: when Richard had been about twenty, he'd quarreled with his father and left for India; his father had died the following year; and Uncle

Albert had returned to England to assume the title and estate. Since Richard had gone to India before Uncle's return, the two had not met until Richard, now in his mid-forties and styled Major Yardley, had come back to England. Then he'd died in Uncle's library.

Those were the bare facts. But several observations and tantalizing questions struck me.

First, had Uncle been aware of his brother's return to England? How long had the Major been back? Had the two men corresponded, despite my aunts' suggestion that there was a dislike between them? Why had the Major been in Uncle Albert's library? And why had he died there?

And then a thought struck me. I wondered why I hadn't considered it before. The most reasonable explanation for Major Yardley's presence in Uncle's library was that he was staying at Uncle's house.

Satisfied at least on that point, I returned to my examination of the rest of my aunts' gossip. They had insinuated that Richard had left England under a dark cloud, born of a disagreement with his father over a young woman, whom the father had deemed unsuitable for his son. But why had he left the country at all? What a rash thing to do! Had he been running from something he'd done? Why had he stayed away from England for so long? Why had he returned now, more than twenty years later? Had he been ill, perhaps dying? Or had he been trying to right some wrong he'd fled from as a young man?

I lingered upon that thought for a moment. If he had committed something wrong in his youth, could my aunts be correct in suggesting that the Major had died not of natural causes but of poison? Had someone murdered him in retribution?

I shuddered. If Major Yardley had been poisoned, was not Uncle Albert the most likely culprit? After all, the Major had died in his house. An unpleasant notion wormed its way into my head. Was that the urgent matter for which Uncle was seeking assistance?

Unthinkable! What possible motive could Uncle have?

I took a deep breath. The doctor had ruled it a natural death. But then again, he would not be the first doctor to declare a death *natural* without checking for a gunshot wound or traces of poison. Even so, Uncle could have had nothing to do with the Major's death. If the Major had somehow met an unnatural end, the reason was most likely to be found in his past.

And that brought my thoughts back to the girl over whom Richard had fallen out with his father. While my aunts said she'd met a tragic end, they'd claimed to be ignorant of the particulars. But regardless, the Major could not have been responsible for her death. She'd died after he'd left for India. Was her death the reason he'd stayed away from England? So why was he back now?

This consideration reminded me of one of my aunts' more sinister suggestions. Could Major Yardley have come to Uncle Albert's house intending to kill him and inherit the title? It was certainly a sentiment my aunts favored. And then, the most surprising thought crystalized: as Uncle had not seen his brother as an adult, could this Major Yardley have been an impostor? It was a rather exciting proposition!

Thrilled by all these tantalizing questions and ideas, and by the feeling that a mystery was bubbling just below the surface stretching back to Major Yardley's youth, I drove on rather fast.

I reached the boundary of Uncle Albert's estate by late afternoon. The farmers were out in the fields, guiding their horses through a sea of gold. As the horses followed their owners, the reaper-binders hitched to them carved neat rows in the wheat. Behind them, farmhands were setting the sheaves into stooks to dry under the last of the summer's rays. It felt as though on Uncle's estate little had changed since the time of Constable, when the artist had painted the English countryside in such romantic detail. The fields of ripened wheat, the gentle breeze, the farmers with their carts, the mellow afternoon light, the church spire of a rural parish behind the distant hills, all served to remind one that here people still lived by the rhythm of the seasons. It was a welcome respite from the feverish energy at home, where the farm work was overshadowed by the wedding.

As I passed through the gatehouse, a park opened up on either side of the drive. It was a pleasant vista of rolling hills. An imposing glasshouse with a tall dome could be seen in the distance. It spoke of generations of keen horticulturists, employing the best designers, and the best gardeners. The eighteenth-century garden plans were still visible in the immaculate gravel paths, the clipped yews lined up like soldiers, the rose enclosure resplendent in bloom. But even so, gardeners could not reach everywhere, and I was glad to see that nature was slowly reclaiming the expansive grounds. Beyond the gardens, it grew green and luscious, wild and untamed, in a constant flux of death and rebirth.

I wondered why I had not visited before. With my time at school, then the war and my brother Charles' death, and then my time in Switzerland and London, I'd had no occasion to be here, I reasoned. But even since becoming his secretary, Uncle had not invited me to his estate. I knew, of course, that with the demands the Royal Society imposed on his time, and the far-flung places his interests in bugs and birds took him, Uncle was rarely home.

As I drove beneath the arching boughs of ancient trees, I found myself musing as to why Uncle was always going on expeditions with the Royal Society. Was he seeking a reason to be away from here?

Soon, Tatham Hall came into view. It was a sprawling Jacobean mansion in red brick, softened by time, with large mullioned windows, clusters of tall chimneys, and turrets topped with ogee copper domes, now turned green.

Wilford, who when at home, served as butler, welcomed me. Upright in stance and character, he was, as always, immaculately turned out and courteous. He led me through a screens passage into the Great Hall.

The inside of the house bore something of the spirit of the wilder grounds outside. The Great Hall, once a grand reception room, now resembled a repository. Cluttered like an overgrown garden, it was as though cabinets and vitrines, Persian rugs, mounted collections of butterflies and beetles, masks, weapons, and portraits had invaded like weeds. The spoils from centuries of exploration had crawled, climbed and twisted around every column, and in the process had covered every surface. But like the gardens, all had a slightly decaying quality. The rugs were threadbare from generations of footsteps; the butterflies were molting; and the portraits were hardly visible under their deep brown patina.

After exchanging some pleasantries with Wilford, and discovering that Uncle was sequestered in his greenhouse, I jumped straight to the matter at hand. "Is the Major's body still in the library?" I asked. I'd half-expected to see him laid out in the Hall.

"No, my lady, the body was taken away by the doctor," he said.

"That's rather unorthodox in the case of a natural death," I countered. "Is there any suspicion of foul play?" I asked cautiously, my aunts' theory about Uncle poisoning the Major nagging in the back of my mind.

"None whatsoever, my lady," Wilford said and cast me a quizzical glance. "Doctor Perkins examined the Major's body and pronounced it a heart attack. According to the doctor, the Major had led a rather gregarious life that was bound to catch up with him eventually."

"Why is the body not laid out here?" I asked. Should not the Major, as Uncle's half-brother, have been laid out in the best room of the house, as was customary?

"The body is to be laid out at the Vicarage," Wilford said.

I nodded, trying to appear as though none of these developments struck me as strange. Everything seemed slightly off, but I shook the notion away. I'd felt this way since this morning, upon hearing of Uncle Albert's hitherto-unknown-to-me brothers. But perhaps Wilford was not the best person to discuss this with, so instead I said, "Who found the body?"

"His Lordship."

"Indeed?" I raised an eyebrow. Was this lending credence to my aunts' theory that Uncle Albert was somehow involved? But rather than giving voice to that possibility, I added. "Poor Uncle. How it must have shocked him!"

Wilford simply inclined his head.

"How long had Major Yardley been back?" I asked.

"He'd been in the neighborhood for about a week," Wilford said, "and not many days longer in England, from what I understand."

"In the neighborhood?" I said, surprised by his phrasing. "Was he not staying here at the house?"

"Indeed not, my lady," Wilford said. His usually steady gaze betrayed some puzzlement. "The Major had taken up rooms at the Inn in the village."

"Really?" The news was unexpected. "Is it not strange that the Major would choose to stay at an inn, rather than with Uncle Albert?" Uncle surely had room to spare.

"If I may be permitted to make the observation, my lady, the two brothers were like strangers to each other. His Lordship, your uncle, was away for much of the time when his father's second family lived here. Perhaps the Major did not feel comfortable being your uncle's guest."

That was rather singular behavior. "But this was the Major's childhood home," I countered.

Wilford made a noncommittal noise, but did not offer anything further.

The mention of the men being strangers brought to mind my earlier conjecture. "Can we be absolutely certain that this man was Major Yardley?" I asked. If he had been an imposter, it would explain why he had elected not to stay at the Hall. It would have become obvious rather quickly that he was not familiar with the place.

"I think there could be no doubt that the man was Major Yardley," Wilford said.

"Oh," I offered in return, disappointed to be robbed so quickly of that rather rousing prospect. "How can you be sure?" I then pressed. Surely the man was a stranger to Wilford as well.

Wilford cleared his throat gently instead of replying. It was then that I noticed the two tall youths in footmen's livery standing sentry by a door leading off of the Great Hall. Though they were staring ahead with studied indifference, nothing prevented them from listening in on our conversation.

"Shall we walk to the library?" I suggested.

Wilford nodded and led the way through a door at the high end.

CHAPTER 5

We proceeded down a long gallery-like passage towards the back of the house. Generations of wild-haired Lord Tathams stared at us in the most unrestrained manner as we walked by their portraits.

"How can you be certain that the Major was not an impostor?" I asked, pursuing my idea. "You've never met the man before, have you?"

"I haven't," he said. "But surely the Major's brothers would have recognized an impostor."

"Yes, of course, his brothers!" I said a little too enthusiastically, having forgotten momentarily about them. "They would have met the Major upon his return to England, of course," I added to cover up my blunder. I felt uneasy revealing to Wilford that I was completely in the dark regarding Uncle's step-family.

"Indeed, my lady," he concurred, but a hint of bemusement crossed his face. Perhaps noticing some of my own confusion, he continued. "The Hon. Eliot Yardley, who is the youngest of the three brothers, is a country barrister, and now resides with his wife at the Dowager's House on the grounds. And the Rev. the Hon. Bernard Yardley occupies the Vicarage with his wife. When the living became available a few years ago, it was within your uncle's right to present it to him."

I tried not to show how surprised I was to learn that Uncle's step-brothers lived on his estate. At least that explained why the Major's body was now resting at the Vicar's house, I mused.

I smiled shyly at Wilford by way of thanks. Like any good butler, he had correctly surmised the source of discomfort and spared me the embarrassment of having to ask for details about Uncle's relations.

"Was the Major's return a surprise to Uncle?" I asked.

"I believe it was," Wilford said. "As far as I know, the Major had made no attempt to contact His Lordship all these years."

"And was his return also a surprise for his brothers?" I inquired further.

"I could not say, my lady."

We walked in silence for a few moments while I worked through some ideas in my mind.

"How odd that Major Yardley should end up dead in Uncle's library," I said. "His sudden return strikes me as rather curious. Especially as it was followed by his sudden demise." Of course, the benign explanation for this—that the Major had returned to England because he was ill and dying—was not as intriguing to me as the possibility of foul play. "The mystery of his return is further compounded by the fact that, as I understand it, the Major left under the cloud of scandal all those years ago," I added, trying to gauge how much Wilford knew about what had transpired here during the Major's youth.

"It was before my time, my lady," Wilford said diplomatically. If he knew something, he was not letting on.

We turned a corner and made our way down a darkly paneled hallway. The portraits of Lords having been exhausted, here we were looked down upon by their wives. For a moment I wondered if the late Lord Tatham's wife was among them.

"Why do you think the Major came back to England after all this time?" I asked, trying a different tack.

"I cannot say, my lady," he said.

I cocked an irritated eyebrow at him. He was the best-informed retainer I knew.

He relented. "I was not privy to their private conversations, but in my presence, the brothers did little more than reminisce about old times." He looked as though he were about to add something, but hesitated.

"Yes, Wilford? Is there something else?"

He paused in his step, and so did I. His expression vacillated for a few more moments.

"Since the Major's return," he said, "several strange events have transpired, though one finds it difficult to imagine how they could be related to his homecoming."

"What events?" I asked, intrigued.

"Break-ins at the greenhouse, and the house," Wilford said, his tone laced with indignation.

"Oh!" I said, surprised. "I thought those had merely been excuses Uncle Albert had fabricated to delay coming to our place."

"Regrettably not, my lady," Wilford said. Though his countenance was quite stoic, a slight furrowing between the brows told me that these events had shaken him.

"What happened, exactly?"

"The first break-in was at the smaller greenhouse, which is your uncle's domain, away from the main greenhouse of the gardeners. The second break-in was not a day later. One of the display cases in the Great Hall was forced open."

I regretted not having taken a closer look at the case when we'd been in the Hall. "Was anything taken?"

"Not as far as I could tell," Wilford said. "But the display case is rather cluttered with curios," he added after a moment, as though offering an excuse.

"And you think the events are connected with the Major's return?" I asked.

"One must be careful not to confuse temporal coincidence with causality," he said rather philosophically, and frustratingly noncommittally.

"No, indeed," I said. And yet, it was rather telling that the break-ins had coincided with the Major's arrival in the neighborhood.

We continued on towards the library.

"And what is your theory about the break-ins?" I asked.

"I have none," he said.

"And does Uncle have some ideas on the subject?"

Out of the corner of my eye, I could see Wilford suppressing a smile. "Several."

Any further probing about those theories, however, would have to wait—we had reached the library.

Wilford pushed open the carved double doors, and as I walked through, I gasped. Uncle's library was something that would make the Provosts of some universities jealous. Late afternoon light streamed through tall windows. It set aglow the golden-brown wood of the inlaid floor and illuminated the towering bookcases lining the walls. A curved staircase to the left of the door gave access to the gallery along the upper level of the library, while a domed ceiling painted with allegories depicting Knowledge triumphing over Ignorance with the guidance of Truth soared above it all.

I walked further in, drawn forth by a pair of enormous globes—one terrestrial, one celestial—resting on intricately decorated wooden bases. A long oak table ran the length of the room. Books lay open, revealing colorful plates of tropical birds. Next to them, journals, their thick pages yellowed with age, displayed inked sketches of the cross-section of various exotic fruits. Letters covered in tightly scribbled text interspersed with diagrams put one in mind of long-forgotten expeditions.

In the alcove of a window, a desk's surface was littered with dried specimens while a magnifying glass mounted on a stand stood expectantly above them. Nearby, the half-open flat drawers of a cabinet housed herbarium pages.

Was this evidence of Major Yardley having searched for something in the library before his death? Though, on closer inspection, a layer of dust had settled over everything, and one was overcome by the impression that a previous Lord had taken books down and opened drawers, and no one had bothered to put the library in order in centuries.

Wilford noticed my roving glance, and as though anticipating my question, said, "His Lordship does not allow us to dust and tidy up here as often as the staff would like. He fears that an important document would be dislodged from its precarious resting place, never to be found again.

Or that the diaphanous wing of a rare specimen might be dusted off."

I nodded. I quite liked it the way it was. It was the manifestation of Uncle Albert's disorderly manner and thoughts.

I followed Wilford to the French doors at the far end of the library. He paused by a green velvet chair. "This is where the Major's body was found," he said, indicating a space on the Persian rug. "He was lying here, just as if he'd slumped off the chair."

"Poor man," I said, the forlorn chair suddenly filling me with grief for this unknown man. "To have traveled all the way back home simply to die."

Wilford nodded solemnly.

"How did the Major gain entry into the library?" I asked.

"I cannot say, my lady," Wilford said. "When I made my rounds last night, the library was empty and the doors to the gardens were locked."

I glanced back at the open drawers and the jumble of books on the oak table, and wondered if the Major had broken into the library.

Wilford shook his head when I posed the question to him. "There was no sign of forced entry this morning, yet the doors to the gardens were unlocked."

"Someone let the Major in?" I asked, surprised.

"I've spoken to the staff, and they've denied any

knowledge of the Major's presence in the library."

Then, I mused, the only other person who could have let the Major in was Uncle. But I didn't voice that inference. My aunts' insinuation rose again in my mind. Had something passed between the two brothers last night?

Pushing that unpleasant possibility aside, I brought my attention back to the space by the green chair. "How long did the doctor say the Major had been dead?"

"Six to eight hours. Which would put his time of death at around midnight," Wilford replied.

"Uncle must have been quite surprised to find the, er, Major here this morning," I said, still trying to understand the situation and Uncle's place in it. I wondered how the old relation had taken the discovery of the body. At least he had the refuge of his greenhouse and his plants to soothe his mind.

Wilford cleared his throat before proceeding. "I was left with the strong impression that the Major's presence here was not entirely unexpected to His Lordship. That he was dead, of course, was certainly a shock," he amended, "but I had the distinct feeling that I was more astounded than His Lordship to find the Major here."

"Indeed?" I said, dread welling up inside me.

He nodded and, oblivious to the apprehension the turn in conversation was causing me, continued, "Perhaps His Lordship's lack of surprise was due to a note that had arrived from the Major earlier in the day yesterday. Upon reading it, His Lordship hurried to the library in high spirits."

I took a steadying breath. The Major had died of natural causes, I reiterated to myself, trying to quiet my anxiety. Uncle had nothing to do with his death. "Given the note, then, should we assume it was Uncle who let the Major in?" I asked, trying to keep my voice level at this startling revelation.

"His Lordship went to bed at his regular time," Wilford said loyally.

I smiled uneasily, but did not object. It would not be the first time Uncle Albert had wandered around after the servants had secured the house and gone to bed.

"This midnight visit is most peculiar," I said, glancing about the library again. "Did Uncle give any indication of what the Major might have been doing here? Was the Major looking for something?" I dared not ask if Wilford had perhaps spied the contents of the note.

"His Lordship didn't say. After finding the body, he was rather evasive and departed for his greenhouse without a word."

"Perhaps it was the shock of finding his brother dead," I said, trying to explain away Uncle's peculiar behavior. Had Uncle drawn himself into some unpleasant affair?

"There is one possible clue as to the Major's purpose here," Wilford said.

"Yes?" I said eagerly.

"There were several books on the topic of Indian plants next to where the Major must have been sitting," he said, indicating a stack on a low table by the green chair.

"The Major is unlikely to have come all this way to consult about Indian plants," I said, disappointed, after throwing a cursory glance at the tomes with titles like *Flora of British India* and *Flora Indica*. With a heavy heart, I conceded it was high time to speak to Uncle Albert about what he knew of the Major's visit to the library. "Shall we find Uncle?" I said.

CHAPTER 6

I paused just outside the French doors and looked at the ground. Were there any footprints that would indicate the Major had met with someone in the library? But with the doctor and servants scurrying about, I could hardly expect to be able to distinguish one footprint from another. Moreover, it had been dry, and there was nothing to discern on the terrace.

"There is one other possibility," Wilford said, observing my activity, "as to who might have let the Major into the library."

I looked up at him sharply. "Yes?" I said as eagerly as a drowning person clutches at a straw.

"The library is also used by Mr. Graves. He is His Lordship's cousin, presently visiting the estate."

Yet another person I knew nothing about! But the existence of Mr. Graves, and his current stay at Uncle's, provided instant relief to my troubled thoughts.

"He's an archeologist," Wilford continued, "interested in some purported Anglo-Saxon burial mounds on the estate. I believe he's also taken upon himself to act as the Yardley family's archivist."

The disdain in Wilford's tone had not escaped me. I wondered what had precipitated it, but I could discover its cause later.

"And you think Mr. Graves could have let the Major in?" I asked, filled with hope.

"He professes innocence on that point," Wilford said. "But he could have left the door unlocked by mistake," he added, rather charitably, I thought.

"And where is Mr. Graves now?"

"Somewhere on the grounds," Wilford said and cast his gaze over the gardens and the park beyond.

Wilford set off down the graveled garden path, and I fell into step by his side. For a while, I walked in silence, lost in thought. Mr. Graves was yet another kinsman of whom I was wholly ignorant. Why was Uncle so secretive concerning these relations? For a moment, the shadows of all these men I'd suddenly learned about, but never met, hovered menacingly about Uncle Albert in my mind. Why was the Major back? What was he doing in the library at midnight? And why was this archivist nosing about in the library as well?

"Wilford," I said, "is it not possible that the Major and Mr. Graves were looking for something, the same thing, in the library?"

"Like what, my lady?"

"I don't know. Some family documents,

perhaps?"

"It's quite possible," Wilford conceded after a moment. "The library houses the family's archive."

"Can you think of a reason why two distant relations might be rifling through the archive?" I asked with interest.

Wilford cast me a sly glance. "My lady, you are not perhaps thinking that there is some family secret the men are, were, trying to unearth amongst the old papers?"

I smiled. "Perhaps. There wouldn't be some family legend about a treasure?"

It was Wilford's turn to smile. "Alas, no. Not to my knowledge. All the treasures the previous Lords brought back from their sojourns about the Empire are displayed quite openly on the walls of the Hall."

I nodded. And while I didn't contradict Wilford, I was not satisfied that the break-ins and the sudden interest in the library were unconnected. I was not convinced that the Major had been looking at books on Indian plants. More likely, he was searching through the same documents as Mr. Graves. But to what end?

"Was the note the first communication Uncle had from the Major since his return?" I asked, the thought suddenly striking me. If the Major was interested in the archives, why had he not communicated with Uncle immediately upon his arrival? What had the Major been doing for a week? Or had he just recently discovered that what he was looking for was housed in the library?

"No, my lady. Upon learning that the Major was in the village, your uncle invited him to tea, and attended further teas at the residences of his brothers. A dinner was also planned."

Down the sloping lawn, I hurried to keep up with Wilford. Close to seventy, he had the stamina and bearing of someone decades younger. As we crossed the estate, I was on the lookout for a figure that could be Mr. Graves, but didn't see anyone about.

We passed by the greenhouse I'd seen from the drive. Its height and breadth reminded me of Kew Gardens. Through the panes, a flurry of activity was visible. Under-gardeners were clearing away dry leaves from plants, prodding the soil, or tying branches heavy with fruit to supports. I could see tall palms reaching for the top of the glass dome, the wide leaves of banana trees, and the sharp tips of a sprawling agave.

"We will find His Lordship in the secret greenhouse," Wilford said as we passed a young man in rolled-up shirtsleeves scrubbing dirt out of a terracotta pot. More were stacked on a trestle table by him. He doffed his cap as we passed.

"Secret?" I asked, intrigued by the name.

"So called because it's rather out of the way and houses some of the estate's more dangerous plants," Wilford replied as we made our way towards a thicket just beyond the edge of the glasshouse. "It was added by Lord Tatham's father, the late Earl. From what I've heard, he had a rather unhealthy obsession with poisonous plants. When one of the village children almost died after breaking into the greenhouse and eating a rather tasty-looking red berry, Lady Tatham, your uncle's mother, insisted that all poisonous plants be locked away in a purpose-built greenhouse."

We ducked under some branches and entered the copse. Dappled light played upon us through the leaves. The winding path became narrower and overgrown as it led us deeper into the woods. Here the canopy thickened, and shafts of sunlight broke through the gloom only occasionally. The air was cool and moist.

Then, quite suddenly, Wilford pushed another branch aside, and we stepped into the bright light of a clearing. In front of us was a small greenhouse, no bigger than a child's playhouse. With ornate ironwork and arched windows, it was like a pretty jewelry box. Woods grew all around it, hiding it from prying eyes. Through the glass, with the sun shining on his back, I could see Uncle pottering about inside.

But a large wooden board marred the front of the pretty glasshouse.

"The break-in?" I asked.

Wilford nodded.

"Was the other greenhouse also attacked?" I

had observed no damage as we'd passed.

"No, my lady."

"How singular," I mused aloud.

Inside the greenhouse, the air was hot, but not unpleasant. A gratifying breeze circulated through the open ventilators along the roof. Uncle was stooped over a plant in a pot, tending to it gently with his knobbly fingers and seemed not to have noticed our entrance.

As Wilford threaded his way between the raised plant beds and potting benches, I couldn't help but note the difference between him and Uncle, as both men were about the same age. Wilford was tall, with an erect posture and a spotless coat. Uncle was hunched and dressed in a gardening smock, liberally smudged with soil and mud. He was humming, as though singing to the plant. In response, his fluffy white hair, which stood around his head like a dandelion clock, vibrated gently with the notes of the love song he was doling out to the tiny shrub.

Wilford cleared his throat as we approached.

"Ah, Caroline!" Uncle cried, looking up. "Glad you are here!"

"How are you, Uncle?"

"Troubled, very troubled," he said, his head drooping forward as though from the weight of all his thoughts.

I nodded compassionately. "This is quite a hidden place," I observed. I didn't want to trouble him quite yet with questions about the Major.

He looked around and chuckled. "Father was always rather put out by having to move his poisonous plants here. He considered having them at the great greenhouse a jolly good deterrent against mischievous children who had a habit of breaking-in and stealing his pineapples. But my mother felt strongly on that point. Father, not to be outflanked, surreptitiously planted poisonous plants throughout the property. One can still find the deadly trail he established, if one is a discerning connoisseur of these things." He touched the side of his nose knowingly. "But some poisonous plants, especially the ones from the tropics, are rather delicate. They cannot survive our English winters without the warm comforts of a greenhouse." He clipped some dry leaves off the stem of the plant he was tending with a pair of embroidery scissors. It had gentle pink flowers growing in clusters.

I eyed the surrounding plants with suspicion. Vigorous green shoots wound their tendrils around string suspended from the greenhouse's metal frames, reaching ever higher towards the light, as though trying to escape. Many of the plants displayed an array of bright berries, from clusters of blue ones to individual red ones, from ones that looked like small plums to others that were like beautiful beads. I reminded myself not to touch any of them.

"Having spent quite some time in India," Uncle continued, not looking up from his charge, "my father, a spiteful man, was rather fond of the idea of Karma. He viewed the poisonous plants hidden about the estate, and those who would succumb to them, as divine retribution. Trial by ordeal, as he liked to say."

"That's rather horrible," I said.

"Well now, we haven't had an outsized number of poisonings," Uncle said in a mollifying manner. "And the locals are weary of tramping through the gardens, so I guess that's a good thing. Though one hears that the woman running the Inn in the village is very accomplished in the art of tinctures and tonics. Apparently she's helped more than one unhappy woman put her husband in his place." He looked up at me and winked.

I frowned. Was Uncle suggesting that a woman in the village was supplying poison to discontented wives?

Uncle returned to fiddling with the flowers of his plant. "One hears that on the whole husbands in the village are particularly well-behaved," he said and shrugged as though the mysteries of married life were beyond him. "A great-aunt of hers was once accused of witchcraft, but that's neither here nor there. I've always imagined that my grounds are the source of plants for the skillful landlady."

"Did the police ever investigate?"

Uncle waved my question away, not lifting his gaze from the plant. "Accidents. All accidents."

I sighed and cast another look around the greenhouse. Broken pots; an upturned watering can; soil spilling out of a torn sack; trowels, shears and secateurs strewn about. My eye fell on the board patching up the broken window. Now was as good a moment as any to inquire about all the strange things that had occurred on the estate since the Major's return. "Is this the state the greenhouse was left in after the break-in?"

Uncle Albert cast me a befuddled glance and then looked about him. At the same time, Wilford shook his head at me, as though to say that nothing here was out of the ordinary.

I smiled. Indeed, on second look, just like the library, this place had Uncle Albert's rather unique touch of chaos. *As in the house, so in the garden.*

"Was anything taken?" Though I wondered how whoever had broken in could have found anything in this mess. And indeed, how could one tell if anything was missing?

"Nothing," Uncle Albert said with confidence after throwing another cursory look around.

"How can you be sure?"

He gave me a scathing look this time. "I've spent every waking hour, and sometimes even slept in this greenhouse over the past fortnight, tending to my specimen for the Worcestershire Flower Show," he said, caressing the pink flowers of the plant he'd been tending. "I'd notice if so much as a leaf went missing."

I very much doubted that, given Uncle's poor eyesight. But I let it go.

"What do you think they were after?" I asked.

"What else? They were here for my prized plant!"

CHAPTER 7

"Who on Earth would be after your plant, Uncle?" I asked, suppressing a laugh.

"Don't be so dismissive, Caroline," he chided. "Despite rallying the entire household to be on the lookout, it appears I haven't succeeded in impressing upon them the magnitude of the situation, and the most criminal activities have been going on right under our noses. I'm glad you are here now to lend a hand."

I frowned. Was he referring to the plant or something else entirely?

"And even if we haven't caught anyone in the act," he continued, "I have at least two culprits in mind."

"You do?" I was curious to hear his thoughts about the break-ins.

"I shouldn't be surprised if it was the scoundrels from the Royal Society!" he declared.

"Why?!" I cried, startled. Though upon reflection, the assertion was not entirely unforeseen.

"Trying to sabotage my entry into the flower show, of course."

Eyeing the pot he'd been lavishing with attention, I judged that it contained the plant in question. "But they didn't take it?" I asked.

"Well, no," Uncle said, his voice a trifle shaky, as though he was beginning to see the weak link in his theory. "Maybe they were just trying to size up the competition. All the chaps from the Royal Society are entering the Show this year."

Though nothing about Uncle's theory made sense, I had to admit that the greenhouse break-in had all the hallmarks of his chums from the Royal Society. "Are any of them nearby?"

"Well, Lord Fetherly is just over the county line and has recently acquired a Bugatti Type 35. Wilford tells me the vehicle isn't road-legal —racing car, you see—but Fetherly is a complete rotter, and I'm sure he would have no qualms about taking it on the by-roads if it meant a glimpse at my entry."

I nodded, delighted to see that Uncle's opinion of his closest friends had not improved. "And your second suspect?" I wondered if he would name Major Yardley.

"The Vicar's wife."

"Indeed?!" I was quite taken aback by the unexpected accusation. I mused for a moment whether she was the wife of his other half-brother, but since Uncle had not brought them up yet,

I asked instead, "Is she also entering the flower show competition?"

"No, she's organizing it," Uncle said gravely.

"What possible reason would she have for breaking in?" I asked, perplexed.

"Well," Uncle said, and acquired the look of a storyteller settling in for a long winter's chat around the fire, "Lord Abington is distant cousins with the King of Denmark, and he got him to sponsor the flower show this year. So in his honor, we have a little bet going—we're trying to see who can grow the most poisonous plant."

I stifled a chuckle at the Hamlet association. Despite their titles and position in society, Uncle and his Royal Society cronies were just a bunch of mischievous schoolboys.

"But the Vicar's wife has been rather vociferous with her objections. Doesn't want poisonous entries, you see." Uncle shook his head at the injustice. "Says we're making a mockery of the Show and of the honor the King of Denmark has bestowed upon it."

"And why did she break in?" I asked.

"She was probably looking for a way to disqualify my entry," he added with a shrug.

"And yet, she failed to destroy the plant, thus leaving you free to enter it into the competition," I said gently, trying to make him see how improbable his theory was.

"Well, when you put it like that, it does

seem unlikely," he admitted quietly. "But that still doesn't explain why we've had a spate of break-ins. They began just as I announced my intention to enter the *Abrus precatorius* in this year's Show." He'd regained some of his confidence and spared me a challenging glance.

I did believe that the break-ins were an indication that someone was looking for something on his estate, but I was certain it was not his plant. "What is so special about your flower, Uncle?" I asked, chiefly to appease him.

"Ah, glad you asked," he said, the sparkle in his eyes and the spring in his hair now fully restored. He pushed the pot he'd been poring over towards me. The plant growing out of it was delicate, with soft, feathery leaves, reminiscent of a fern. Its slender stalk had coiled itself around a central support, displaying clusters of pale-pink flowers, not unlike those of the pea.

"It's so fragile-looking," I said. I had the urge to touch its leaves.

"Ah, but so deadly," Uncle said and chuckled as I snatched my hand away. "The bet is as good as settled in my favor. In the tropics, where the *Abrus precatorius* is native, it grows strong and tall. I've seen it in the wild in Ceylon. It's an impressive, tangled beast. This one is just a youngster. Hasn't had its first seeds yet." Uncle cooed over it fondly, as though it were an infant about to sprout its first tooth. "It's the berries that are so poisonous.

Many times more deadly than ricin." He cast me an appraising look and smiled upon perceiving my alarmed expression. "Even Major Yardley was duly impressed."

Uncle's mention of the Major took me by surprise. I'd been avoiding asking about him for fear of upsetting him. "He was interested in your plant?!" I said.

Uncle nodded enthusiastically. "Yes. Though having lived for so long in India, he should have been quite familiar with it. Well-known among the natives there..."

"Uncle," I said, interrupting him, and proceeded cautiously with a theory that challenged his. "You say the break-ins coincided with your announcement regarding the flower show, but didn't they also begin upon the Major's return?"

Uncle chuckled. "Caroline, even I don't think that Richard would come all the way from India to steal my plant!" He shook his head at me in disbelief. "Poor soul," he added.

"But what if the Major was not interested in your plant, but something else?" I said carefully.

"No, that's where you are wrong, Caroline," Uncle said rather animatedly. "He wrote me a note. Asked about my plant specifically."

I eyed him doubtfully. What could the note have possibly said to make Uncle reach such a conclusion?

"I didn't particularly enjoy the man's company,"

Uncle was saying. "He'd bored us over tea with his army stories." He'd lifted the skirt of his smock and was rummaging through the pockets of the house jacket underneath as he spoke. He proceeded to pull out a handkerchief, pencil stubs, string, a lorgnette chain with a fob, but no lorgnettes, a small pocketbook, several glass vials, viscous liquid sliding down their sides, stoppers, and a handful of crumpled papers. "Aha! Here it is," he said triumphantly, unfurling one of the sorrier-looking slips of paper. He smoothed down the creases and furrows and handed it to me.

I glanced over the note and read out the most significant part. "I'd like to talk to you about the rosary pea you're growing, in private. Signed, Richard." I looked up in astonishment. "This is the note from the Major?" I was rather surprised by its contents, to say the least.

Uncle nodded. "Couldn't deny anyone the pleasure of learning about *Abrus precatorius*, that's the rosary pea he mentions, so I invited him to the library that very evening. Dashed off there myself to prepare all the literature I had on the subject. Laid out all six volumes of *Icones Plantarum Indiae Orientalis* by Robert Wight for him. Splendid illustrations. I was rather pleased to find he'd been reading one while he..." Uncle faltered and glanced towards Wilford.

"Indeed," Wilford said, picking up his cue after a moment. "A book on Indian plants lay beside the

Major's body, as though he'd been reading it."

I shook my head in disbelief. Nothing made sense. Despite all the evidence, I remained unconvinced. "Why would the Major want to know more about your plant?!" I countered. "How did he even hear that you were growing it?"

"Why, I told them all about it," Uncle said innocently, "when I had Richard, Bernard and Eliot, and their wives over for tea."

I looked at him curiously. He spoke about his relations as though I knew about them. Upon reflection, he'd probably forgotten that he'd never mentioned them to me. I put that thought aside and returned to the matter of the Major. "And then what happened? Was it you who let the Major into the library last night?"

"Me?" Uncle's voice squeaked, and he contrived to look hurt by the insinuation. He then cast a glance at Wilford, who had the presence of mind to appear deeply absorbed in a plant. Uncle became reticent. "I...went down to unlock the French windows, as you say," he began after some fiddling with a dry leaf, "must have been about eleven, after Wilford had made his final rounds and the staff were in bed." He cast a swift glance towards the valet. Wilford had by now moved to the other end of the greenhouse, and was hidden from view by some bushy creepers. Uncle relaxed a bit. "I meant to wait for the Major, but I spotted a monograph on *Franklinia alatamaha* that I had been looking for.

Saw it peeking out from under a stack of books I'd moved while searching for tomes on Indian flora. I...I became quite absorbed by it, and took it up to bed with me...and fell asleep. I'd quite forgotten about the meeting with Richard, you see," he said sheepishly. "I didn't think about it again until the morning. And then, when I rushed down, I found him dead."

"How dreadful!" I said.

Uncle looked crestfallen. His head drooped even lower, while his hair appeared to have gone quite limp.

"But it wasn't your fault," I added quickly. "It was a heart attack."

Uncle nodded, looking somewhat unconvinced.

I was about to press on with my questions when a sharp clink followed by the tinkle of glass breaking interrupted us from where Wilford had retreated to.

"Oh, Wilford!" cried Uncle, as though knowing precisely what had shattered. "Not the distillation equipment!" He shuffled in the direction of his valet. Something in his energetic manner told me that he was relieved to be rid of the topic of the Major for a moment.

"I apologize, Your Lordship," the valet said solemnly.

I followed Uncle. Behind the screen of creepers was what looked like an alchemist's laboratory—a tangle of coiled glass tubes and interconnected flasks. At one end, a burner sent a crystalline liquid boiling; at the other, an amber liquid collected in a flask.

"What is this used for?" I asked, watching the dark fluid spiral through the contraption.

"To extract a plant's most precious essence," Uncle Albert said after concluding his inspection of the apparatus and ascertaining that Wilford had only broken a test tube.

"You mean poison?" After all, that was the essence of poisonous plants, and we were surrounded by them.

"The dose makes the poison, Caroline," Uncle Albert said rather sagely. "While certainly some of these plants could kill,"—he gazed about the greenhouse—"a lower dose could cure. A rather Alice-in-Wonderland conundrum..."

While Uncle was thus philosophizing, ideas began swirling in my mind. "Could whoever broke into the greenhouse have been after the poisons you extract?" I asked. My aunts' warning had come back to me like a Greek chorus.

A flush crept up Uncle Albert's cheeks. He avoided my gaze. He then cleared his throat and touched some of the apparatus gingerly. "Well, now. The crux of the matter is...it would appear that such delicate chemical work is not my forte. Apparently, I'm more of a theorist when it comes to these things..."

He appeared overcome with feeling and

gestured towards Wilford to fill in the gaps.

"Dr. Perkins, the local physician," Wilford began, "has questioned His Lordship's ability to apply in practice the considerable theoretical knowledge he undoubtedly possesses. In short, your uncle has come perilously close to poisoning himself more than once, and the doctor has expressly forbidden him from experimenting with further distillations."

"Dr. Perkins had the impertinence to tell me," Uncle Albert cut in, "that my purifications were imprecise and, while they posed no danger to anyone else, he's concerned for my health. After several near misses, I'm under strict doctor's orders to brew nothing stronger than tea. The man's a fool." Uncle released a valve, filled a flask with the amber liquid, and raised it towards me. "Tea, Caroline?"

I declined with a shake of the head. He took a contented sip.

I stared at him. "But, Uncle, don't you see?! Whoever broke in here might have been after your poisons!" The break-in was suddenly beginning to make sense.

"No, Caroline," Uncle said with a knowing air. "That's not possible. The doctor took away all my distillates weeks ago."

CHAPTER 8

Wilford gently reminded us it was time to make our way back to the house to dress for dinner.

It transpired that the rest of Uncle's step-family had been invited to dine with us that evening. I had anticipated that my stay at Uncle's would be of some duration, since I'd surmised that I would not be able to shepherd him to our own abode as quickly as Mother had hoped. Thus, I had packed for most occasions that could arise over the next few days, even the Major's funeral.

We were taking the long route to the house, as Wilford deemed the shortcut through the woods too perilous for Uncle, owing to roots and stray branches.

"This morning, upon learning of Robert's death," Uncle was saying, "Julia decided that the family needed to get together, *to discuss matters*, as she said."

I did not know who Julia was, but did not interrupt him. While speaking, Uncle was also negotiating a protruding root.

"Moreover," he continued, task accomplished, "the news that you were driving down has created some excitement among the women. Perhaps they look forward to hearing about the fashionable sleeve length this season in London, or some such thing." Uncle waved his hand dismissively. I smiled. He had a slightly old-fashioned notion of female conversation. "You've never met them, have you?" He looked at me quizzically, as though the omission was my fault. I shook my head. "Yes, I suppose you haven't," was all he supplied in return.

I looked at Uncle expectantly, but he didn't seem interested in elaborating.

"Julia is Mrs. Eliot Yardley," Wilford, who was walking behind us, said discreetly. "The barrister's wife."

I offered him an appreciative smile over my shoulder.

"The chaps are all right, but the wives are a fright," Uncle continued, unperturbed. "Julia in particular. Likes to boss people about. Seeking the magistrate's appointment, God help us." He shuddered. "Very active sort of female. Always poking her nose into other people's affairs. Campaigning on a platform against petty crime. I wouldn't put it past her if, once in office, she has me up before the Bench for poaching on my own land." He gave a short chuckle.

I listened intently, as I was rather curious about

Uncle's half-brothers and their wives, and was looking forward to meeting them at dinner. But the prospect did not distract me from reflecting upon what I had learned in the greenhouse. Ideas that had merely been diaphanous musings before were beginning to take shape.

One of the biggest revelations so far was that Uncle's "secret" greenhouse had housed extracts from poisonous plants until recently. While the doctor may have dismissed Uncle's skills as inexact, he'd nevertheless thought it prudent to take away the distillates, lest Uncle poisoned himself. This suggested that though crude, the extractions could be harmful, perhaps even fatal.

Could whoever had broken into the greenhouse have been looking for the poisons? But then, they must not have known that the poisons had been removed.

"Uncle," I said, "is the existence of the secret greenhouse known among the populace of the village?"

"Oh, yes," Uncle nodded emphatically. "I should say so. Youngsters are always poking about in the vicinity, curious, noses pressed against the glass, leaving snotty imprints. Have been since my father's time, when he set up the distillation equipment in there."

I nodded. Not such a secret greenhouse, after all. Anyone local might have known about the poisonous plants in the greenhouse. The Major, who had grown up on the estate, even more so.

"And how long was it again since the doctor got rid of your distillates?" I asked.

"A fortnight." Uncle's voice laden with regret.

"Was it generally known that the doctor had taken your, er, experiments away?"

"I should hope not!" Uncle said sharply. "It would be scandalous for the doctor to engage in such idle gossip."

I smiled at Uncle. His ardor was, perhaps, a way to mask his worry that if word of the doctor's actions got out, his reputation as a plant expert would be tarnished. But I conceded that it would be unbecoming for a country doctor to be indiscreet about the foibles of the local Lord. So, if that were the case, I mused, the Major, or anyone else in the neighborhood familiar with the contents of the greenhouse, might not have been aware that the poisonous extracts were no longer there.

"And what did the doctor do with the extracts?" I pressed on.

"Put them in his dispensary, I should think," Uncle said.

I very much doubted that, as the extracts were nothing short of poison, but didn't voice my objection. "Has there been a break-in at the doctor's recently?" I asked instead.

Uncle cast me a sly look. "Why all these questions, Caroline?"

"I'm merely trying to work through some ideas," I said. "Well, has there been a break-in at the surgery?"

"Not that I know of," Uncle said.

I sighed. This only proved that perhaps whoever forced their way into the greenhouse didn't know the poisons had been moved, if indeed that was what they had been looking for. Intentions would have been so much clearer if the break-in at the greenhouse had been followed by a break-in at the doctor's. As it were, I had no proof that the greenhouse malefactor had been after the poisons at all. Moreover, there was another problem with my theory—the subsequent break-in at the house. What was there in a greenhouse that, when not found in it, would make someone look for it in the house? It was quite a riddle. Perhaps the culprit thought the poisons were moved to the house? But why look for them in the curio cabinet, of all places?

I could not see the connection between the two break-ins. I was certain I was missing something. Were the two break-ins perpetrated by two different people?

The motivation behind the greenhouse break-in was clearer to me. Either, if Uncle were to be believed, it was the Vicar's wife or his chums from the Royal Society going after his plant. Or, and this was more likely, someone was looking for the poisons, such as the Major, for some unknown reason, or the skillful tincture-maker woman from the Inn.

But did any of these people have a motive to break into the house? It was more plausible that an entirely different person had rifled through the curio cabinet. It was rather strange, however, that these events occurred a mere day apart.

I shook my head in frustration. I needed more clues. Once again, my thoughts returned to the conundrum of the Major in the library.

Slipping my arm through Uncle's, I said, "So you never discovered what the Major wished to talk to you about."

He paused in his step and frowned at me. "The plant, Caroline," he said rather testily.

"Uncle," I began gently, but firmly, as we resumed our walk, "did it not strike you as peculiar that the Major wanted to talk to you about your plant, alone, in your library, after dark?"

He looked at me with clear, guileless eyes, and blinked a few times for good measure. "What do you mean, Caroline?"

I proceeded carefully, both in our stride and metaphorically. It would be difficult to convince Uncle that not everyone was as interested in his plants as he was. "I believe the note was a ruse on the Major's part to gain entrance into the library."

"Poppycock," said Uncle. But he frowned slightly and then turned his gaze to the surrounding parkland.

"I think the two break-ins are connected," I said, offering up my theory. "But they have nothing to do with your plant."

Uncle was silent for a while, as though considering my assertion.

"Help me reconstruct the Major's movements since his return to the village," I said.

Though I was speaking to Uncle, I fully expected Wilford to supplement any omissions. I hoped that going over the Major's activities might elucidate his motivations for requesting a clandestine meeting with Uncle.

"Well," Uncle began, "he arrived about a week ago and took up rooms at the Inn."

"Was that not rather singular?"

Uncle shrugged. "Military men are set in their ways. More comfortable in austere surroundings, I suppose. And we were never close."

"And how did you come to hear about his return?"

"I suppose one of his brothers told me. Perhaps the Vicar."

"And then?"

"Upon learning of his return, I invited him and his brothers to tea, as was expected of me, as Margaret informed me—"

"The Vicar's wife," interjected Wilford.

I nodded appreciatively. "And all was normal?"

"As normal as could be expected. Though

Margaret got all huffy when I began telling them about my entry for the flower show," Uncle said.

"And then, the break-in at the house happened the evening of the tea?" I asked. Something had clicked in my mind.

"Yes," Uncle said, with a slight hesitation.

"But then...when did the break-in at the greenhouse occur?" I asked, trying to make certain I had reconstructed the sequence of events correctly in my head. "Was it not before the break-in at the house?"

"Yes?" Uncle said, this time even more doubtful.

"The day before the tea at the house, my lady," Wilford supplied from the back.

I nodded, satisfied. "Therefore, the break-in at the greenhouse occurred before you spoke to the Major and his brothers about your plant!" I said somewhat triumphantly.

Uncle did not respond.

"I believe that whoever broke into the greenhouse did not know that you were growing that plant, Uncle," I clarified.

He walked on in defiant silence.

"But I suspect they broke into it looking for your distillates," I said.

As expected, this mollified Uncle, and he lifted his head a little higher.

"But then, what puzzles me," I continued, "is that this was followed by the break-in at the house.

Have you any idea what the villain might have been after?"

"None," Uncle said.

"Could whoever broke into the house have been looking for the same thing as the Major and Mr. Graves?"

"The Major and Mr. Graves?!" Uncle exclaimed. "Like what?" he added a bit more shrewdly.

"I don't know," I admitted. "Something valuable."

Uncle shook his head.

"What is Mr. Graves searching for in the library?" I said. "If he's interested in those Anglo-Saxon mounds, what is he hoping to find in the family records?"

Uncle sniggered. "Many of our ancestors have been fascinated by those mounds and have taken a shovel to them. I believe he's looking at any records of what might have been recovered."

"And?"

"I know for certain that at least one of those mounds is a rubbish heap from the time the medieval castle stood here, before the Jacobean Hall was built. It is said to contain the refuse of a rather ruinous four-month visit by Henry VIII and his retinue." Uncle chuckled dryly.

"So not all are Anglo-Saxon mounds?"

Uncle shrugged indifferently.

I vaguely wondered if Mr. Graves had unearthed

something more significant than Tudor rubbish, and had communicated it to the Major.

"Is it possible that the Major and Mr. Graves were in correspondence with each other?"

"In correspondence?" Uncle asked, incredulous. "They did not know each other. Mr. Graves is from my mother's side of the family."

I nodded, but was not entirely convinced that there was no connection between the two men. Why had their visits coincided? And it was rather telling that the break-ins happened while the two men were on the estate. But I could get a better measure of the family archivist at dinner.

"What was the Major doing between the day you had tea with him and the day you received the note?" I asked, determined to establish a clearer picture of the Major's time before his death. "It's my understanding that a few days had passed between the two."

"Well, we had more teas. Once at the Vicarage and once at the Dowager's House," Uncle said. "And a dinner was planned, but we had to postpone it because the Major was not well."

"Not well?" I asked, startled that no one had mentioned this before. "You mean the Major was ill?"

Uncle nodded. "I was, in fact, rather surprised to receive the note from him yesterday. He was supposed to be confined to bed. Had been, for a couple of days."

"What was wrong with him?" I asked, breathless. A strange tingling sensation was crawling up my arms, and I shuddered.

"That doctor is a fool," Uncle pressed on, as though he had not heard me. "Heart attack! Pshaw! Pale and weak, anyone could see the Major suffered from some tropical disease." He then paused and looked at me, as though a thought had just occurred to him. "I hope it's not catching!"

A thought had just occurred to me too, though of a rather different nature. The idea had been there before, lurking—Uncle's poisonous plant, the Major's note about it, the break-in at a greenhouse filled with lethal distillates—but I had been avoiding giving it my full attention, perhaps because I disliked the notion of my aunts being right. Or perhaps because I feared Uncle's involvement, however inadvertent. After all, Wilford's description of Uncle's evasive behavior upon finding the body had perplexed me. But now, in light of the Major's illness, the question could no longer be ignored: Had the Major indeed been poisoned?

CHAPTER 9

The most awkward phase was over. Uncle's step-relations and I had made our introductions earlier, while we were gathered in the drawing room, awaiting everyone's arrival. The stilted manner of our exchange, and the ill-disguised interest with which we examined one another, made it clear that each party felt slightly uneasy at having remained strangers for so long. The Major's death only compounded the discomfort, as names were traded alongside condolences.

As dinner progressed, however, we began to feel more at ease—or perhaps it was the wine—and we were now sitting quite amicably around the dining table. Conversation had naturally turned to the death of the Major. I listened intently, searching for hints of whether anyone shared my misgivings about the Major's sudden demise. But discussion had so far been limited to the man's funeral, and Bernard Yardley, the Vicar, was telling us about the arrangements he'd made for it in two-days' time.

Wilford had been kind enough to give me a brief background on each brother. The Vicar, after being ordained, had spent many years in India, on a mission among the poor. He'd ministered among the untouchables, the lowest caste. Before departing on his mission, he had married Margaret, the daughter of a minor, but respectable, member of the local gentry. The Vicar had returned to England about five years ago, when the living in Uncle's village had become available.

I glanced sideways at the Vicar, who was sitting on my right, as he spoke. His deep voice appeared to keep his listeners in thrall. His face was kind, but weathered, perhaps owing to his time in India, and deep lines framed his warm brown eyes. He still had a full head of sandy hair, though now liberally threaded with gray. And despite his middle age, his lean figure still bore some signs of an athletic youth.

His wife was sitting opposite me, and I turned my attention to her next. Though I understood her to be the same age as her husband, she looked older. Perhaps she was simply care-worn. Her features were plain, and she wore a modest black dress with a high neck. She'd styled her graying dark hair in a soft wave.

They made a slightly incongruous couple. While both were reserved, her husband had the air of someone naturally shy who worked to overcome his timidity through kindness and thoughtfulness. His wife, on the other hand, struck me as someone whose reticence was a cultivated detachment. Perhaps it was simply a shield she'd forged during the years spent among the Empire's most destitute. How strange it must feel to be now privy to the worries and grievances of the English village parishioner. And yet, of all the family, she appeared to feel the Major's death most keenly. A certain paleness, quite striking against the black dress, overcame her each time her husband spoke of his brother.

"I still can't believe Richard is dead," the Vicar said after a pause.

An assenting murmur passed around the table. I searched the faces of the rest of the diners, wondering if anyone would take this cue to comment on the Major's health prior to his death. Was I alone in thinking there had been something peculiar in his symptoms? Was no one else suspicious that the doctor had declared the Major's death a heart attack despite the man's acute illness?

My glance paused on Mr. Graves, Uncle's cousin. While Uncle shared few features with his step-brothers, the resemblance between the two cousins was remarkable. Mr. Graves had Uncle's flyaway white hair, stooped stance, and dogged devotion to a rather niche hobby. In the drawing room before dinner, Mr. Graves had kept to himself, retiring to the shadows. I'd failed to learn anything meaningful about him. And now, he was sitting at the other end of the table, quiet, ignored by the other guests, and left out of the conversation. I could not tell if he was listening closely or completely oblivious to it.

"I can hardly believe it myself," said Eliot Yardley, drawing my attention away from Mr. Graves.

Seated beside the Vicar's wife, Eliot Yardley was perfectly placed for my observation. A successful country barrister, according to Wilford, he had his sights set on taking silk and, ultimately, becoming a judge. Though also according to Wilford, the barrister's rather gregarious nature was viewed as something of a hindrance in that respect. As a testament to a more comfortable life, perhaps, the barrister was heavier set than the Vicar. His face was fuller and less lined, but his fair hair was thinning at the crown. He exuded affability, and his eyes were intelligent, even sparkling with something akin to mischief, when not eclipsed by grief.

"I—" Eliot Yardley began, but then stopped himself after glancing at his wife, remaining silent for a few moments. He then chuckled to himself, and said, as though changing tack, "Remember how upset Father got when Richard broke the window of the small greenhouse with a slingshot?" He was perhaps addressing the Vicar, but appeared to be speaking to the room.

I perked up at the mention of the greenhouse and wondered what had prompted him to recall this incident. And then a wisp of a thought floated through my mind: could the greenhouse window have been broken this time round as some act of nostalgia? Or retribution? Was there any significance in the reoccurrence?

"No slingshots for us from then on," Eliot Yardley went on, almost speaking to himself. "Absolutely forbidden. One risked severe punishment if caught with a slingshot in his pocket. But we liked running around and aiming at things, didn't we?" He chuckled lightly and looked at his brother.

"Strange," the Vicar said thoughtfully after a moment, "Father did not mind, and even encouraged shooting at living things. But one would get quite a hiding from him if one broke a vase or a window. Certainly taught us the value of material things versus life," he added.

I cast a quick glance at Uncle Albert. Did he share his brother's opinion of his father? Had his father been as uncompromising with him? But Uncle was looking down at his plate.

"That's when we had to switch to peashooters," Eliot Yardley continued. "Oh, I expect we were quite a nuisance in those days. I remember one of our favorite games as kids was to aim at the girls we liked. We'd practice on the train from school, coming home for the holidays. We'd shoot balls of paper at the workers along the train line." He chuckled. "You were still running with us in those days, remember, Julia?" he turned to his wife. "But you could dish it out as well as anyone. Quite a good shot."

His wife laughed nervously, as though embarrassed by this childish recollection. "Oh, that was such a long time ago."

Julia Yardley was sitting on the other side of the Vicar, so I could not see her face at the moment, but she had made a strong impression on me when we'd been introduced before dinner. Unlike her sister-in-law, Julia was high-spirited and self-assured. Flamboyant, even, as much as one could be in a small village. She had abundant blonde hair, styled quite expertly in a stylish bob, and a well-preserved face. The only thing preventing her from being called handsome was her rather tall, sturdy frame. Her smiles were full of teeth, which lent them a domineering quality. I could see that she would make a perfect magistrate, much to Uncle's chagrin. She gave every impression of managing her husband closely, but the easy smiles he cast her way suggested that he didn't much mind. According to Wilford, she was also a local girl, who'd grown up with an aunt and uncle.

"Eliot was the best shot among us," the Vicar said, giving into the reminiscence. "And could reach rather far."

"And my target was always Julia," his brother said and laughed heartily.

The Vicar's wife had remained quiet during this

exchange. I glanced at her, wondering whether she too, as a local child, had run about the estate with the brothers. The polite, faintly fixed smile she wore, however, suggested that she had never taken part in those games.

"You may not believe it now, Lady Caroline," Eliot Yardley said, and I returned my attention to him, "but my wife was quite the tomboy in those days. And then, one summer I came back for the holidays, and she'd transformed into a beauty." He cast her a loving look.

The momentary elation the remembrance of their youth had brought forth now passed abruptly into silence, as though the men suddenly recalled that one of their childhood playmates was dead.

"Poor Richard," Eliot Yardley said after a moment. "He was Father's favorite. Could do no wrong."

"Until he did," the Vicar added.

His brother nodded. "That is why his fall from grace was so total and complete."

"And why Father was so hard on him," the Vicar said.

Eliot Yardley took a sip of wine. "And all of us boys aiming to please Father, clamoring for his attention and his favor. Lord knows why, he had no love to give us and little else to leave us."

Though there was no malice in the barrister's voice, and the remark seemed to be made quite innocently, without meaning to cause offense, I glanced quickly at Uncle—the son who'd received everything his father had to leave. Though perhaps he too had received no love. Uncle, however, seemed entirely absorbed in dissecting a snap pea on his plate with his dinner knife.

"It was quite a surprise to see Richard in London after all those years," said the Vicar's wife. Her voice was high and strained, as though she'd hurried to think of some way to divert the conversation.

"You saw him in London?" I asked innocently. I stabbed nonchalantly at my own pea pods, but in truth, I was quite interested in this piece of information.

"Oh, yes," Eliot Yardley said. "We ran into him at the offices of the family's solicitors. It was quite a shock, to be sure. Never told any of us he was back." He chuckled, as though at a good joke, before catching himself and taking another sip. He didn't elaborate further.

Not wishing to appear nosy, I smiled demurely, but I was desperate to learn more. Why had they all been at the family's solicitors? Why had they been surprised to see the Major there? And why had the Major not told his relations he'd returned to England?

"I wonder what made him come back?" said Julia Yardley.

"He was probably in need of money," her

husband said offhandedly. He then looked up at me and added, "We draw an allowance from an annuity our father left us. The sum is rather modest, and it was felt that keeping the assets together, rather than splitting them between the three brothers, would yield a better return." This rather candid revelation was spoken without embarrassment, in the businesslike tone of a man who relished practical details.

"You don't have to sugarcoat it," Julia Yardley interceded. "Your father was a difficult man, even at the best of times. He set up those terms so that he could control you and your brothers even from beyond the grave."

"Julia!" her husband exclaimed, drawing himself up as though in warning.

"One of the stipulations," she continued unfazed, leaning forward to address me around the Vicar, her voice booming, "is that each brother has to collect his allowance in person at the solicitors' in London. It's such a bother for such a small sum."

"Julia, this is hardly appropriate," the Vicar said.

"It was a condition the old man added to punish Richard for running away to India," Julia Yardley hurried on, determined to speak her mind. "It was his way of trying to force him to come back to England. But Richard did not capitulate."

The Vicar's wife sighed. Perhaps this was the

conversation she had been trying to avoid.

"So the Major has not been able to collect all these years?" I asked. I was careful to appear quite disinterested, as though merely keeping up the conversation out of politeness, but ideas were fermenting in my mind.

"A rather tidy sum had collected for him, I would imagine," the barrister said.

But I would learn no more for the time being. The Vicar, perhaps judging that enough had been said on the subject, changed the conversation back to the funeral arrangements. Discussion moved on to the refreshments to be served at the reception following the funeral, and over dessert, Uncle's relations speculated about who from the village might attend.

Unfamiliar with the names mentioned, I turned to my thoughts instead. How did these new snippets of information fit in with what I'd already suspected about the Major's death? Had the Major returned because he'd been in need of money? Did money have a hand in his death? Had someone killed him to keep him from collecting the accumulated annuity? And if money were at play here, I mused, could the Major's death be connected to something I'd discovered from Wilford just prior to dinner?

The scraping of chairs brought my attention back to the dinner table. It was time to leave the gentlemen to their drinks.

CHAPTER 10

Margaret Yardley, Julia Yardley, and I withdrew to the drawing room. It was a suitably grand space appointed with all the paraphernalia of wealth and comfort—a great marble chimneypiece, portraits by old masters, even one of Henry VIII, gilded flourishes, plush carpets, deep chairs, exquisite crystal, polished silver, and delicate china. The effect, however, was spoiled somewhat by the lopsided application of botanical prints among the oils. One detected Uncle's touch.

As Margaret Yardley poured coffee, I turned my thoughts to what I'd learned from Wilford just before dinner. After I'd returned from the greenhouse, and before changing for dinner, I'd gone to the Great Hall to examine the curio cabinet. I had been wondering whether a closer inspection of its contents might not supply me with an answer to my riddle—what was that which one would look for in a curio cabinet, after failing to find it in a greenhouse?

The cabinet had been as expected. Large, and glass-fronted, its shelves were overflowing with a jumble of the most unlikely things—ivory carvings, exotic shells with silver-trimmed edges, glittering mineral specimens, Ancient Egyptian artifacts, Chinese antiques, Indian objets d'art, all girdled with a smattering of gold coins, ostentatious rings, and miniature jeweled boxes. It had been impossible to ascertain whether anything was missing. There was no telltale empty spot. The only indication that anything was amiss had been the splintered wood where the lock had been forced.

As I'd come back down to dinner, however, Wilford had approached me, just as I'd been making my way to the drawing room to join the rest of the guests. It transpired that he had news bearing on the item missing from the cabinet.

"One of the under-maids, Lily, who only occasionally services the Great Hall," Wilford had said, "was helping the parlormaid, Hannah, put the downstairs in order for the dinner party. Lily had not been in the Great Hall since the break-in, and it was only this afternoon that she had the opportunity to view the display cabinet. It was then that she realized something was missing from among the objects—a bracelet."

"A bracelet? Why had no one noticed it gone before?" I had asked, surprised by the omission.

"I must admit, my lady," Wilford had said, "that with the cabinet filled as it is with singular pieces, a mere bracelet is easy to overlook. Hannah, who does the Great Hall, didn't notice the bracelet gone because she avoids looking into the cabinet on account of the rather menacing ceremonial masks—from the Shang dynasty, I believe—so it wasn't until Lily that anyone realized anything was gone."

"Observant girl."

Wilford had concurred. "Lily clarified she'd taken particular notice of the bracelet before because it had been the prettiest of the objects in the cabinet."

"And could she describe it?"

"Silver, with white stones as large as pearls, and a lovely silver clasp, as per Lily. It was the clasp that had drawn her to the bracelet. Rather intricate, the bracelet is something an Indian princess would wear, as Lily put it."

Thanking Wilford and making a mental note to leave a coin for Lily upon departure, I had gone in search of Uncle. Cornering him discreetly just prior to dinner, he, however, had been unable to tell me anything about the bracelet, not even if it were valuable. Like Wilford, he'd admitted to never noticing it. "There are several important pieces in there, and the rest is simply a collection of trinkets from around the Empire." He'd waved his hand dismissively.

The only thing Uncle had been able to tell me with any certainty was that he had not placed the bracelet in the cabinet. Thus, its presence there dated at least to his father's time, if not earlier, meaning that the Major might well have been aware of its existence.

Initially, I'd wondered if the bracelet had been of some sentimental value to the Major, if indeed it had been him who'd stolen it. But now, in light of the conversation during dinner, I wondered if the Major had taken it because he'd been in need of money.

But why was I so certain that it was the Major who had taken the bracelet? I mused while I sipped my coffee. Was it because its disappearance coincided with his return? But it also coincided with Mr. Graves' visit.

I gazed at the two women sitting across from me over my cup. At least I could rule out Uncle's other brothers and their wives from the list of suspects. They'd had years of opportunity to remove it, had the bracelet held any value for them.

As usually happens, the new clue raised more questions than it answered. How did the break-in at the greenhouse fit in? Why steal the bracelet instead of simply asking Uncle for it? I was certain he would not have refused. If the Major had taken the bracelet, was he killed for it? And where was the bracelet now?

Margaret Yardley was staring into the distance. Catching my glance, she appeared to will herself back to the present and gave me a small smile. Perhaps I'd imagined it, but I felt as though the gesture masked a deep sadness. The feeling was only heightened by the weariness in her eyes.

Julia Yardley was examining me and my dress quite openly. I believe she found me wanting. She offered an unabashed grin in return. Her own mourning number was rather extravagant, with a voluminous bow across the hips.

"You must excuse my husband's frankness over dinner," Julia Yardley said. "He does like to speak his mind. A professional quirk, if you will."

I smiled politely. Julia Yardley was perhaps unaware that she shared her husband's trait.

"Only men would think that Richard's return was about money," Margaret Yardley said quietly. It seemed as though she was voicing the thoughts that had been occupying her. "Though, I must admit that all three brothers have always been rather preoccupied with money and status. Perhaps because they had grown up with all the trappings of wealth and money around them, but in the end it was denied to them."

She cast a glance about the room. I nodded, thinking of James. It was a complication faced by all younger sons.

Julia Yardley opened her mouth to object, offense driving her eyebrows up, but Margaret Yardley continued, "Even my husband is not immune. Being a clergyman, he tries so hard to fight against greed. I believe that was what drew him to the missionary life, to deny himself that which he longed for. But he, like other men, is weak. Just like Eliot wants to be a judge, my husband aspires to become a bishop. About the only thing his noble birth is good for."

"Margaret!" Julia Yardley finally protested. "What has come over you this evening?! You're making a fool of yourself in front of our guest." The smile Julia Yardley tossed me was rather frazzled.

I lowered my gaze to my cup to spare her any embarrassment. Like her, however, I also wondered what had prompted the candor among Uncle's step-family. Perhaps the Major's unexpected return and death had stirred old ghosts. And though I shared some of Julia Yardley's scruples, I was not willing to forgo this opportunity to learn more about the Major.

"Why do you think the Major returned?" I asked Margaret Yardley gently.

She considered the question for a moment, looking at the cup in her lap. I could feel her sister-in-law glaring at her, but no doubt a cognizance of the difference in our stations prevented her from objecting to my inquiry.

"I don't know what brought Richard back to England," Margaret Yardley said. She then raised her head and looked at me as though she'd made up her mind about something. "You know, when we met him at the solicitors' I had the impression that he'd wished to avoid us. We were late for the meeting, we'd had to catch a later train. And he'd made his appointment with the solicitors for the hour after we'd been expected there."

"That's preposterous," Julia Yardley objected, unable to help herself. "Why would he wish to avoid his family?" The question echoed my own.

Margaret Yardley shrugged and looked away. "He'd grown apart from his brothers, perhaps. He had not really kept in touch with them. Perhaps he felt guilty for staying away all those years."

"Guilty?" I asked, the word catching my attention.

Margaret Yardley turned to me sharply, her eyes wide. "Perhaps that's not the right word. Perhaps he simply felt uneasy seeing his brothers after twenty years." She paused and adjusted her cup on its saucer.

"Please go on," I said.

She considered her cup for a moment. Then, as though wishing to get the words out before she changed her mind, she said hurriedly, "I don't know what brought him to England, but I know what brought him here, to the village."

This time I dared not interrupt her with a question. I hoped that her sister-in-law would not cut in either, but a swift glance in her direction, and the quizzical look on her face, told me that she was just as eager to hear what Margaret Yardley might reveal.

"Love," Margaret Yardley whispered.

Love?! I wanted to say, but resisted.

"He'd stayed away because of love, and came back because of love," she said. Her countenance had once more taken on that detached, faraway quality. "You should have seen the look on his face when he saw me in London," she continued, turning to me. "His expression left me in no doubt as to why he then came to the village."

I stared back at her, aghast. Was Margaret Yardley suggesting that the Major had been in love with her and that it was this love that had kept him away from England and had ultimately engendered his return?

"He noticed the necklace I was wearing, a small locket. I saw the moment he recognized it," she continued, and touched the place where the ornament rested under her dress.

I was about to ask if she meant a bracelet instead, but stopped myself. The bracelet had gone missing only after their meeting in London.

"It was hers, you see," Margaret Yardley said. "I could see the thoughts that were going through Richard's mind. Where did I get it? Why did I have it? Why wasn't it buried with her?"

The unexpected trajectory her story was taking confused me. "Whose was the locket?" I said barely above a whisper.

"Alice's," was all that Margaret Yardley said.

I turned to Julia Yardley, hoping that she would offer some explanation, but she was staring at her sister-in-law in astonishment.

"That locket you wear all the time was hers?!" Julia Yardley said, sounding exasperated. "Surely, Margaret, that cannot be healthy. You always did have a strange obsession with that girl. She was pretty, to be sure, but you know class and good breeding have always counted for more. Especially with the Yardley boys." All the bluster was gone from her voice, replaced by pity for her sister-in-law.

"Who is Alice?" I dared ask, but I had a pretty good idea. She was the girl the Major had been in love with. The one he'd left behind. The one who'd died in tragic circumstances.

As Margaret Yardley seemed overcome by memories, it was Julia who answered my question. "Alice was a local girl, the daughter of the innkeeper. Richard was in love with her. He wished to marry her. But his father would not have it. She was very pretty, I'll grant you that. But nothing could overcome the fact of her low birth. Richard was forbidden to marry her. So, he left for India in protest. He knew he was hurting his father by leaving. His father regarded him as the favorite among his sons. Tall and handsome. Perhaps it was wise of Albert to be ensconced in a faraway corner of the Empire during this time," she said and cast me a mischievous look reminiscent of her husband's. "Anyway, I know all of this through hearsay. I didn't witness any of it. I was away from the village when Richard went away. And then, I suppose Alice could not cope with being abandoned by him. All the rumors, you know, in a small village, and she took her life. Drowned in the lake. Left a note, didn't she, Margaret?"

Margaret Yardley shuddered. "I think Richard came to the village as atonement," she said.

"What do you mean, Margaret?" Julia Yardley asked.

"Did you not notice all the questions he was asking about Alice and her death? Spoke to the doctor about her as well. I think he felt guilty for having been hot-headed in his youth and abandoning her. By punishing his father, he'd only really hurt her. I think that's the real reason he stayed away all these years. He felt guilty about her death."

Any further discussion, however, was interrupted by the entrance of the gentlemen.

CHAPTER 11

As the men walked in, their dour expressions suggested they'd been discussing something disagreeable.

Uncle's head hung in the dejected manner he'd adopted when I'd ventured that the Major had not been interested in his plant. He shuffled to a wing chair and sank sullenly into its worn red upholstery. The chair received him as though embracing an old friend.

I looked reprovingly at his step-brothers who had pulled up chairs near their wives. Had the men done something to upset Uncle? Had they continued to pursue the topic from dinner and discussed money and inadequate inheritance?

Mr. Graves, as though unconcerned with the family's drama, separated from the group, and commenced examining the pictures in the room at a leisurely pace, hands clasped behind his back.

"You took rather a long time," Julia Yardley observed, addressing her husband. "What kept you?"

The Vicar sent a dark glance at the barrister, who appeared to cower under this warning glare for a moment. But then a change came over him, and he pulled himself up and thrust his chest forward.

"Now, look here," Eliot Yardley said, scowling at the Vicar in return. "I was silent during dinner on this point, but I have to speak my mind." His face was rather red, and I wondered if he'd overindulged in brandy.

He motioned to Wilford for a drink, who placed a glass of whisky-and-soda on a low table next to him. For a moment, the barrister ran his finger over the edge of the glass, as though struggling with a decision, then he leaned back in his chair, crossed his legs, and raised his face to us.

"I've mentioned the matter briefly to the men, and in speaking about it to you all, I'm going against Bernard's advice. And Albert doesn't look too happy with my decision either," he added, glancing at Uncle with a rueful smile. "But I'm a man of the law, after all, and if I'm right, this is a serious matter that has to be investigated."

"Oh, Eliot," Julia Yardley said, her voice heavy with disappointment. "Must you?" It was clear that she knew what he was about to say.

Her husband nodded an acknowledgment of her objection, but proceeded nonetheless after reaching for his glass and taking a sip. "With Bernard planning for the funeral, I think it's an important matter to discuss. I was thinking today back to your correspondence from India." He turned to the Vicar. "Remember? About those cases of poisoning and deaths while you were there?"

In lieu of a reply, the Vicar leveled a thunderous look at his brother. The Vicar's wife stood completely motionless, as though afraid to take a breath.

"And then I looked up the matter in a book," the barrister went on, unperturbed. "I consulted Major Ramsey's *Detective Footprints*." His tone was light, as though he had been carried away by the thrill of his discovery. But I could not have been the only one who appreciated the gravity of what he was saying, or suspected where the barrister was leading.

"Of course, it was Albert having talked to us about that plant of his, the rosary pea, that put me in mind of the book," the barrister went on. "There are several chapters devoted to it. Now, Bernard probably knows this as he ministered among them, but for those of you who don't, the rosary pea is employed by the Chamar—that's the lowest caste, the untouchables—in some unsavory business. You see, the Chamar are leatherworkers. They take the hides of dead cattle, cure them, and fashion them into shoes and such. But relying on Nature to take its course, by way of age or disease, is not an effective way to meet demand, especially when the British arrived demanding boots and saddles. So, to speed up the supply, the Chamar began resorting to killing cattle. But it's bad business to kill a cow in India. Sacred, you see. So if the Chamar were to kill a cow, they'd better employ a method that is almost undetectable."

He nodded and took another sip. I cast a quick look around the room. All were staring at the barrister with various degrees of horror on their faces.

"That's where Major Ramsey's book comes in," Eliot Yardley went on. "He was the Bengal Superintendent of Police at the time. Cattle began to die in great numbers. Baffled the authorities. No sign of illness or foul play. No mark on the skin whatsoever. It was Major Ramsey's job to investigate, but it wasn't until some of the culpable Chamar were captured that the method used to kill the cattle came to be known. Fascinating stuff. The Chamar make a paste from the red berries of the rosary pea, the same one Arthur was telling us about, and push the poison under the animal's tongue. Once poisoned, the animal becomes ill and dies in a few days. By the time it dies, the place where the poison was administered has healed. All signs of it are gone." He took another sip of his drink before continuing. "But here is the crucial point: the Chamar use the same poison to assassinate men. The victim simply falls ill for a few days and dies."

A bolt of morbid excitement shot through me. Was that how Major Yardley was murdered?

"That's just horrible!" Julia Yardley cried, color high on her cheeks.

Eliot Yardley nodded approvingly at his wife's exclamation. "It is," he said pensively. "I don't blame the good doctor for missing the signs. To this day, no test has been devised to detect this cunning poison. But all the signs were there." He turned to the Vicar. "You must have seen them?"

"Must I?" his brother asked sharply.

"The cases recorded in Major Ramsey's book are from the 1880s, years before you were in the Bengal, of course. We were not even born when Major Ramsey was conducting his investigations," Eliot Yardley added with a chuckle. "But I daresay, according to your letters, the practice still went on while you were there."

"What on Earth are you getting at, Eliot?" the Vicar cut in. His voice held a steely note, and his soft eyes had become unyielding.

Next to him, his wife cast him a furtive glance. A shadow of fear passed over her face. Her reaction struck me as uncalled for, and it was difficult to surmise its source. It appeared as though she was afraid for her husband. Or, was she in that moment, perhaps, frightened of him?

"I believe Dr. Perkins made a mistake with regard to Richard's death," the barrister said simply. "With Richard becoming suddenly ill and then dying a few days later...I believe Richard was poisoned."

A cry escaped from the Vicar's wife. Her face, already pale, had gone positively bloodless. It occurred to me that, out of all of us, the barrister's assertion had come as a surprise only to her. The men had heard Eliot Yardley's suspicion during the after-dinner drinks, his wife appeared to have been privy to it at home, and I had reached a similar conclusion.

For a moment, no one noticed Margaret Yardley's pitiful condition. The Vicar was glaring at his brother. Uncle appeared to have surrendered completely to his gloominess and had sunk even deeper into his chair. And Julia Yardley had her eyes narrowed at her husband, a flush creeping up her face.

My glance finally rested on Mr. Graves. He'd halted his perusal of the art and had perched on a chair in the shadows at the far end of the room. His eyes were trained on someone, though it was difficult to say on whom.

I had conducted these observations in mere moments, and presently I realized that as an innocent bystander, I should be shocked by Eliot Yardley's unexpected statement. I sprang into action. "That's horrible!" I said, feigning disbelief. It was all I could come up with in the spur of the moment.

"My apologies, Lady Caroline," said Julia

Yardley. "Eliot," she addressed her husband with a warning tone, "I told you not to mention this. The idea is preposterous, pure speculation. All you are doing is upsetting people. Where others see illness, a barrister sees murder," she said, turning to me. "There are many reasons why a man might die in a library, but to a barrister, it can only be murder." Her flushed appearance betrayed her utter embarrassment at her husband's claim. She tried to smile, but failed, and in the end just bared her teeth. "Where would anyone even get this poison?" she asked her husband.

"Haven't you been paying attention, Julia?" Eliot Yardley said, though not unkindly. "From the plant Albert is entering in the flower show competition."

Hearing of his plant abused in such a manner, Uncle revived a bit, and he sat up in his chair. "I say!" he protested.

I was equally rankled by the insinuation. "You're not suggesting Uncle Albert had anything to do with the Major's death?" I said. Uncle had the least motive of the family to kill the Major. Though at the moment, I couldn't think of what motives the others might have.

But it seemed that Uncle didn't need my help in defending himself. His face had acquired a determination I'd rarely seen before. I was certain I was glancing at the vestiges of Uncle as a young man. "You are absolutely wrong on this point,

Eliot," Uncle said in an assured voice. "Except for the specimen in my greenhouse, there are no *Abrus precatorius* growing on this estate. England is far too cold for this species. I did my bit during the war. With the shortage of coal, I didn't heat the greenhouses. Well, I didn't heat the small greenhouse; the large one had specimens far too valuable to be left to die in the cold. Sometimes I rationed coal in the house to keep the large greenhouse at the optimum temperature." He paused and looked around in confusion.

"The rosary pea," I prompted.

"The point is," Uncle continued with restored vim, "the rosary pea I'm growing arrived just last month as a cutting from a fellow I correspond with in India. It has not produced any seeds yet, and it's the seeds that are poisonous. I'm entirely innocent of Richard's death."

"Oh, Albert," Eliot Yardley said quickly, "I'm not saying that it was you who poisoned him, old chap. I didn't mean to imply that it was you at all. It was only that your plant put me in mind of the method. I'm only saying that Richard was poisoned with the rosary pea."

"Those are strong allegations," the Vicar said.

"No, no," Eliot Yardley said, appearing taken aback. "I'm not accusing anyone here." He had the look of a man who'd expected his theory to be met with a different response. "Lord knows, we haven't seen Richard in over twenty years," he added.

"What motive could any of us have? And this poison takes days to act. Maybe he was poisoned in London. Or even while he was sailing back to England."

But I feared that the barrister's protestations did not ring quite true. I wondered whom he suspected. Since he'd given considerable thought to the manner in which the Major was poisoned, he must surely have conjectured as to the culprit. Was it anyone in the room? Was that why he'd brought up the subject with his family first before going to the police?

"It would appear that Margaret had some cause to object to Albert growing a poisonous plant for the Show," Julia said, and threw a sly look at Uncle.

I glanced around, speculating whether anyone would take this opportunity to mention the break-in at the greenhouse. If the Major was indeed poisoned, that seemed to me as the most likely source of the poison. Though on reflection, all the poison had been taken away by the doctor before the break-in.

"I hope you don't share this theory with anyone outside the family," the Vicar addressed his brother threateningly. "You have no shred of evidence for your theory. The scandal will be disastrous. Think of your career."

"Eliot, dear," Julia Yardley said, "you've upset enough people. I think it's time for us to go." Her tone left no room for objections, and she extended a firm hand to assist him to his feet.

As the party broke up, Wilford and I took Uncle Albert gently by the elbows, to help him extricate himself from the cushions of his chair. Uncle's faithful retainer and I exchanged a meaningful glance, encompassing all that had transpired during the evening, but remained silent.

"Listen, old chap," Eliot Yardley said as he passed Uncle, "what was Richard doing in the library?"

"No...no idea. Didn't even know he was there until this morning," Uncle said and ran a casual hand through his hair. He was perhaps trying to appear suave, but instead came across as flustered. I looked at him curiously. Why was he attempting to be cunning?

"Oh, Caroline," Uncle said, leaning on my arm, as we proceeded down the corridor from the drawing room in measured steps a while later. "If this becomes a police matter, they'll surely take my plant away. But I know the poor thing had nothing to do with Richard's death. It's entirely innocent."

I patted Uncle's hand. "I'm certain they'll do no such thing. And anyway, if the Major was indeed poisoned, there are probably a dozen other plants around the estate that could have been used." I was thinking of all the species my aunts had named.

We'd reached the foot of the staircase. Uncle looked around. Satisfied that no one was about, he said, "I think I gave them all the slip." He chuckled.

"No one would guess that Richard had come to speak to me. Glad I never mentioned the note to any of them."

Was Uncle engaging in all this subterfuge in order to protect his plant? I mused.

"Have a good night," the Vicar said from behind us, startling us. "I came back to fetch Margaret's purse," he added, and lifted a small beaded bag.

Had he overheard us? I wondered.

As we made our way up the stairs towards the bedrooms, Uncle became once again morose. "Oh, Caroline," he said. "I feel terrible. I could not tell them about Richard coming to see me. If they hear that I fell asleep, they'll accuse me of failing to help him. Poor chap, what if I had indeed been able to help him?"

There was nothing much I could say to assuage Uncle's feeling of guilt, though I found it misplaced. The Major's killer was the guilty party.

"There is one other thing," Uncle said as we reached the top of the stairs. "I have a feeling I'm forgetting something. I have the strongest notion that Richard left something for me. But now I can't remember what it is."

"The note?" I offered.

Uncle shook his head. As he still couldn't recollect what that something could be after a few moments, we bid each other goodnight.

I turned back and looked down the stairs. The hall below was now plunged into darkness, but I had the strongest feeling that someone was hiding in the shadows.

CHAPTER 12

I couldn't sleep, and I wondered whether anyone else who'd been present at dinner would be able to either. Surely, there were conversations going on currently in the Vicarage and the Dowager's House reviewing the events of the evening.

What did the late Major's relations make of Eliot Yardley's declaration that Richard had been poisoned?

Certainly, there was some evidence to support his theory. In the days prior to his death, the Major had been feeling unwell. This, coupled with the proliferation of poisonous plants on the estate, had led me to suspect foul play as well.

If Uncle's protestations were correct, however, the poison could not have come from the rosary pea. Then, why had Eliot Yardley been so certain that it had? Had the idea suggested itself to him merely because of Uncle's entry into the flower show? And upon consideration, further complications presented themselves. Why had the doctor not noticed that the Major had been poisoned, if indeed he had? Was it because the rosary pea poison was as undetectable as the barrister claimed? And how had it been administered? Surely the Major would not have allowed anyone to slip poison under his tongue.

I had to admit that until one knew what poison was used, one could not even fathom the method employed to deliver it to the victim.

But there had been something else in Eliot Yardley's assertion this evening. It appeared as though he'd been set on implicating the Vicar. The barrister's reference to the Bengal, to the Vicar's mission there, and to the letters the Vicar had exchanged with him regarding poisonings in the region, were clearly intended to intimate that the Vicar had knowledge of the rosary pea and its lethality. What had been the barrister's objective? Had he been trying to accuse his brother of murdering the Major?

I mused for a moment about the poisonings in India that Eliot Yardley had referred to. Had these occurred among the natives, or had they happened among the British? And how had the Vicar and his wife been implicated in that sad affair? It had not escaped my notice that they had reacted rather sharply to the barrister's allusion to these events. Had the Vicar's involvement been only professional, or had something more personal transpired?

As I had no way of obtaining answers to these

questions at present, I proceeded to speculate about a possible motive for the Major's murder. Two reasons had emerged—love and money. With regard to money, prior to his death, the Major had been to London to collect a rather large sum. More than twenty years' worth of annuities! One had no way of knowing what the pitiful—as Julia Yardley had put it—annual income was, but even the smallest amount compounded over twenty years would be substantial. What had the Major done with the money? Where was it now? One hoped in a bank.

There was one other clue that suggested the murder might have been about money—the stolen bracelet. Had the bracelet been valuable? Had the Major taken it? Had he been killed for it?

Or had the bracelet held sentimental value for the Major? Had he been a sentimental man? His abrupt flight from England, and unannounced return certainly suggested an impetuous nature.

These thoughts inevitably brought me to Margaret Yardley's belief that the Major had stayed away from, and eventually returned to, the village because of love. No one had disputed the fact that he'd been in love with Alice. But why had he left her so readily behind when his father had forbidden their marriage? Had going away to India been part of a secret plan between the lovers? Why then had the girl taken her life? What were the rumors in the village that Julia Yardley had mentioned? Had the rumors driven the girl to her death? There was usually only one reason unmarried girls took their lives.

Had Alice been with child?

A shudder passed over me. Surely not. The Major would not have been so cruel as to leave her to her fate. But what if he hadn't known? Or worse, what if he had left despite knowing? Was that why the Major had stayed away from England and his home for twenty years? Was Margaret Yardley correct in suggesting that he'd felt complicit? Was his death, after all, a retribution for past sins?

Thoughts about what Margaret Yardley knew with regard to Alice's relationship with the Major, and her death, led me to consider the most singular revelation of the evening—Alice's locket. I found myself agreeing with Julia Yardley's assertion that keeping the locket and wearing it was rather curious behavior. Was this conduct born out of an unhealthy obsession? Was that anomaly what had upset the Major upon perceiving the locket in London?

What was the locket's true significance to the Major? And to Margaret? Had seeing the locket truly given the Major the impetus to come to the village? Or had Margaret Yardley invested the occurrence with an outsized meaning? Perhaps the Major had been planning to come to the village and visit his family all along.

There was no doubt, however, that once the

Major had returned, he'd asked questions about Alice and her death. What had he been trying to learn that he did not know already? One would have assumed that his brothers had related the tragic events to him in correspondence soon after they'd occurred.

And then, another thought struck me. I'd almost forgotten about it. Alice had been the daughter of the local innkeeper. Why had the Major chosen to stay at the Inn, with the girl's mother, rather than with his family? Did he blame his family for the girl's death for some reason?

I spent some time going over these questions and thoughts, and reviewing the events that had revealed themselves so far. First, there were the events of the past: the Major's desire to marry Alice, his father's opposition, the son's flight to India, and the girl's drowning. And then, there were the events of the present: the inadvertent meeting of the brothers in London, Margaret Yardley wearing Alice's medallion, the Major's return to the village, his questions about Alice's death, the break-in at the greenhouse, then the house, the missing bracelet, the note to Uncle, and, finally, the Major's death.

I could envision how some of the events fit together, but could not arrange all of them in a meaningful picture. Were they glimpses of a single crime that culminated in the Major's death? Or was I grasping at the unconnected threads of several transgressions?

And what was I to make of the Major's request to speak to Uncle about his poisonous plant just prior to dying? Did the Major know he'd been poisoned? Did he know he had only hours to live? Did he know who'd killed him?

Suddenly, the most unpleasant thought struck me—was there an antidote to this poison? Had the Major wanted to see Uncle because he believed the old relation had an antidote? Was it possible that if Uncle had discovered the Major sooner, he could have saved him? Was that why Uncle was feeling so guilty for forgetting the meeting with the Major?

Poor Uncle.

In the morning, however, I found Uncle to be in a perfect mood. Gone was his gloominess from the previous evening. He was sitting in the breakfast room, humming a little tune, dissecting his kippers with a touch of flourish that hinted at a lightened mind. The room seemed to reciprocate his mood. East-facing, the sun was streaming through the tall windows, bouncing joyfully off the marigold wallpaper and the polished silver.

"Good morning, Caroline," Uncle said cheerily. "How did you sleep?"

"Well enough," I said, while I helped myself to eggs from the sideboard. "I spent quite a bit of time going over the events from dinner, but I must have fallen asleep at some point."

I eyed Uncle quizzically as I took my seat at the table. What could have precipitated this change in his mood?

"Ah, yes," he said sagely. "My mind was also troubled as I prepared for bed. And then I decided to see if I could locate a copy of the book Eliot mentioned in the library. Father was quite the fastidious collector of publications dealing with poisonous plants. And sure enough, there it was, just where I would have expected it to be, between *The Chemistry of Common Poisons* and *The Poisoner's Handbook*."

He chewed contentedly for a moment, while I wondered what about the book had lifted his spirits.

"As poisons go, *Abrus precatorius* produces quite the perfect toxicant," Uncle continued. His voice was laced with something akin to pride. "There is no test that can detect the abrin toxin in the body. And the symptoms are quite the same as any other acute illness: kidney failure, heart failure," he listed these while waving his fork around in the air. "Very astute of Eliot to pick up on the symptoms." He nodded approvingly.

I still failed to comprehend why these rather macabre peculiarities of the poison delighted Uncle, and I said as much.

"Don't you see, Caroline," he said, "with a poison that potent, there was nothing anyone could have done for poor Richard."

I smirked. Now I understood. It absolved Uncle of any responsibility he might have felt for the Major's death. Unless his plant was shown to be implicated, but I didn't mention this.

"Rather sorry that it happened to the fellow," he continued, "but once the poison was administered, death was unavoidable. Though I'm still not convinced that it was the rosary pea that did him in. Where would anyone get it?"

"Could someone have received the berries from India?" I asked. "Just like you received your cutting."

"Yes, I suppose that's possible," he said. He paused to consider the matter. "But why would anyone do that? No one else shares my interest in horticulture around here."

I nodded. It was a valid point. The Major's poisoning appeared not to have been premeditated, or, at least, not planned well in advance. How could it have been? No one had known that the Major had intended to return to England. Or perhaps someone had?

"But not to worry," Uncle said. "There are plenty of other deadly plants around the estate. It could have been any of those, really. But that still presents us with a problem. The poison of the rosary pea is easy enough to extract—simply crush the seeds to get at the fatal pulp inside—but who would have the botanical knowledge and chemical expertise to synthesize the toxins from foxglove or monkshood?"

Who indeed, I wondered. Except for the woman from the Inn. About to make a comment along those lines, I caught Uncle glancing lovingly towards the oriel window. It was only then that I noticed that his prized plant was sitting on a small mahogany table in the alcove. "Taking precautions?" I asked in jest.

"Rather!" Uncle replied in earnest. "I received a communication that Mr. Graves was lurking in the area of the secret greenhouse early this morning. One of the under-gardeners reported him to me. I don't think they like him much, on account of his making all those exploratory holes in the lawn. So, I had the boy fetch the plant. It's bound to be safer here, by my side, where I can see it, with all this criminality going on."

I smiled at Uncle and his slightly bewildering order of priorities, but inwardly I mused about what business Mr. Graves could have had near the greenhouse early in the morning. He didn't join us for breakfast. Was he reticent by nature, as archivists tend to be, or was he avoiding company because he was hiding something?

The rest of breakfast I spent pondering how best I might corner the elusive Cousin to engage him in conversation and perhaps learn more about his purpose for being here. Short of stalking the grounds in hopes of meeting him, however, I could think of no other clever ploy. But as Uncle's estate was rather large, roaming aimlessly did not recommend itself as a productive way to spend the morning. I had other plans.

CHAPTER 13

After breakfast, I went in search of Wilford. Upon discovering him in the butler's pantry, we spent a few minutes discussing the events of the previous evening. But while he agreed with my conjectures, he had little else to add. As he had not been in service here during the Yardley brothers' youth, he could not provide any insight into undercurrents and motivations.

There was one matter, however, that he was well-placed to address. The doctor's decision not to look further into the cause of the Major's death perplexed me. "Wilford, what is your opinion of Dr. Perkins?" I asked.

"Dr. Perkins is well-respected," Wilford said. "I have not had the occasion to avail myself of his professional services, but I've enjoyed a number of convivial evenings in his company at the village inn. We share a common interest in philately. It is my impression that he has a high regard for Lord Tatham's standing in the community. Taking away your uncle's experiments was done with the utmost cordiality and privacy. I believe the doctor did not wish to cause His Lordship any embarrassment over the matter."

"I mean, is he a good doctor?" I said. "In light of Eliot Yardley's assertions that the Major was poisoned, is it likely that Dr. Perkins could have missed any obvious signs?"

"He is considered a capable, caring man. He is indeed known to be quite restrained in his diagnoses, for which he is well regarded in these parts."

"So he's not the type of doctor to write off a death as a heart attack if there are signs of poisoning?"

"Perhaps professional skepticism prevented him from speculating about the Major's death beyond the available evidence. He is also a local man," Wilford added after a moment. "A friend of your uncle's brothers since childhood, as I understand." There was a glint in his eye. "If I may be so bold as to propose a plan of action, my lady. Perhaps a visit to the doctor's surgery might allow you to form your own opinion about him? It might even present you with an opportunity to inquire about his reasons for declaring the Major's death as natural."

"But I'm not ill," I said with disappointment. "What pretext could I use?"

"A mild subterfuge might be in order."

I raised a conspiratorial eyebrow.

"I believe headaches are a popular ailment

among young ladies of good breeding," Wilford offered.

I wrinkled my nose. "I'm unlikely to traipse all the way to the doctor's with a headache."

"No, my lady." He was contemplative for a moment, and then brightened. "The latest issue of *The Country Gentleman's Gentleman Companion* contains a rather informative article about the rise of allergic afflictions among city dwellers visiting the country. The article laments the decline of resilience in the younger gentry and supplies a number of remedies the conscientious retainer might employ to lessen the discomfort of guests to the countryside burdened with such maladies."

"But I don't suffer from allergies," I said. "Will not the doctor see through the deception?"

"The article is quite specific about the symptoms associated with the complaint, describing them in detail so that the well-trained servant would recognize them and be in an advantageous position to advise upon a course of action and relief. One of the symptoms mentioned, if I may suggest, is a reddening around the eyes and nose. I believe the desired effect could be achieved through the judicious application of rouge."

I smiled.

Prior to setting off for the doctor's, I presented myself to Wilford, who pronounced the effect perfect. Thus prepared, I drove off to the village.

While the makeup was sufficient to deceive the doctor's secretary and admit me to his surgery, my disguise was not enough to fool the doctor. So in the forthright manner of country doctors with busy practices, Dr. Perkins asked my true purpose for visiting him.

"Absolutely baseless," he replied when I sought his opinion regarding Eliot Yardley's theory. I stopped short of questioning why the doctor had failed to propose the hypothesis himself. "Yes, Mr. Yardley came to talk to me about his conjectures early this morning. But, as I told him, Richard died of natural causes, not a scratch on him. Well, except for a minor cut behind his ear, and that was a few days old."

"But if he was poisoned, there would not be any physical marks on him," I countered.

The doctor regarded me over his spectacles. He was a compact man of about fifty, in country tweeds, with closely cropped grizzled hair. True to Wilford's description, his manner was calm and deliberate.

"Yes, quite," the doctor said. "But there was absolutely no indication of poisoning. Poisons leave behind telltale signs: bitter almond odor, blue lips. There was nothing to suggest that the Major had been poisoned."

I thought the doctor was protesting rather too much. Why was he so against the idea that the Major might have been poisoned?

"It is my understanding that the Major had been unwell for a few days," I said.

"And why he didn't come to consult me is beyond me," he parried. "Lady Caroline, without being able to prove anything, it would be counterproductive to stir up trouble. As a doctor, I am naturally cautious. And as a country practitioner, I am well aware of what gossip can do to one's reputation in a small village. I gave Eliot Yardley the same warning I am about to give you. No one would benefit from idle gossip. It would only cause trouble for the family."

I nodded. It was clear that I wasn't going to get more out of the doctor regarding the Major's death. But I could not make out the doctor. He appeared to be a reasonable man. After all, he had taken away Uncle's distillates. And yet, he so stubbornly refused to admit that the Major could have been poisoned. Was he protecting someone? If so, who? Or was he indeed a cautious man, reluctant to point a finger or raise alarm without evidence?

But perhaps he could be of help in another way.

"I believe you are a local man," I said. "Did you know the Yardley family well in your youth?"

"Oh, yes," he said. "I'm a near contemporary of the Yardley brothers. The younger ones, anyhow. Your uncle, Lord Tatham, was out of the country for most of that time. Since taking over the local practice, however, I've had the pleasure of getting to know him rather well. But I'm afraid that with your uncle's penchant for exotic plants, my visits have not always been of the social kind." He smiled. There was a hint of humor in his eyes.

I smiled back, and I felt that an understanding passed between us. I was certain he was referring to Uncle Albert's near-disastrous forays into organic chemistry.

"If you knew the brothers well, perhaps you also knew Alice?" I said. I didn't want to waste the doctor's time skirting the point.

He regarded me quizzically for a moment. "I knew her. Everyone did. I believe every young man around here was secretly in love with her." He chuckled lightly. "What makes you ask about her?"

"I gather the Major was interested in learning more about her death. I heard he came to see you. If it wasn't about his illness, I wonder if it was about Alice."

He scowled in the direction of his waiting room and sighed. Perhaps he was lamenting the village's tendency towards gossip. "He did come to see me. I was probably one of the first people he visited. He asked me about Alice and the events that led to her death, but there was little I could tell him about it first-hand. I was up north, doing my housemanship at the time."

I considered for a moment how many people had been away at the time of Alice's drowning—the Major, Julia Yardley, and now the doctor.

"I heard about the accident in a letter from my

mother," he added.

"Accident? Not suicide?" I asked.

Dr. Perkins gazed at me over his glasses. "It was established to have been an accident."

"But I was under the impression that local opinion held that Alice had taken her own life," I said.

"The inquest reached a different conclusion."

"I presume you purchased this practice after the previous doctor retired?" I said. "Did he have any records on Alice?"

Dr. Perkins nodded. "Dr. Graham was the local doctor at the time and the attending physician. He was called upon to examine Alice's body and submitted a written report to the coroner. Because Richard asked me, I went through the archived files and looked at the case notes. Since this is public knowledge, as presented during the inquest, I have no objection sharing it with you. Death was recorded as accidental drowning. There was some bruising on the head—but that supports the accident theory," he added quickly when he perceived my surprise. "Alice most likely slipped and hit her head, causing her to lose consciousness and drown."

"But could someone have hit her on the head instead?" I said, roused by the revelation. My thoughts had quickly moved from the theory of suicide to that of willful murder.

The doctor did not reply immediately. "Dr.

Graham's notes make no mention of any doubt with regard to his conclusion," he said after a few moments. "But I suppose it would be difficult to say whether the bruising was sustained by a blow or a fall."

"And was this the type of information the Major was looking for when he came to speak to you?"

"Yes, Dr. Graham's report appeared to confirm some theory he had formed."

"What theory?" I asked, though I was certain the Major had drawn the conclusion I had, that Alice could have been murdered. I wondered what had prompted the Major to start looking into the matter in the first place.

"Richard didn't confide in me," the doctor said.

"Do you know how long after Richard's departure Alice drowned?" I asked.

"No more than two weeks, I believe."

"And was there any other information in the notes about Alice's health? Anything unexpected?" I was trying to ask if she'd been with child. Though if she had not taken her own life, that was now less likely.

"She was in perfect health," he replied, leveling me a stern look.

I considered what further insight the doctor might be able, or willing, to offer. "Since you knew the Major as a young man," I said, "do you have any explanation as to why he would abandon Alice?"

"I've wondered about that myself," the doctor admitted. "He was a strong-tempered youth. Impulsive. Passionate. They made quite a lovely couple. She was fair, with a beautiful smile. Quite extraordinary. People talk of radiance. She had that." The doctor spoke with a touch of wistfulness. I wondered if he'd been one of the young men in love with Alice.

"And yet, Richard left her," I said.

"I cannot explain his actions. But his father, the late Lord Tatham, was a very difficult man to get along with. Perhaps Richard simply wished to get away from under his control. I'd like to think that he would have come back for Alice after he'd made a career in the Army. Had she lived."

A thought occurred to me. "His father must not have been happy with Richard. I doubt he would have bought his Army commission. Do you know who did?"

"Your uncle, I believe," he said.

I smiled. I should have known.

And then a different notion struck me. "These young men who were in love with Alice, do you think some of them would have pursued her after Richard left?"

"She had a bright future ahead of her," he said, and spared me a bitter smile. "What a wasted life. Yes, I believe she could have made a good marriage, even without Richard."

I considered the doctor. Was he alluding to

himself?

The doctor glanced at the clock and told me he had patients to see. I rather liked his direct manner. I took my leave, thanking him for his time.

On the way out, however, something caught my attention. I dropped my glove, and while retrieving it, I stole a closer look at one of the books on his desk. It was *Pharmacographia Indica*. My school Latin and Greek sufficed to interpret the title. I darted a cautious glance at the doctor. To my surprise, he was observing me closely. Had he seen me reading the title of his book?

"When the Major came to see you, did he already exhibit signs he was ill?" I asked, the idea just occurring to me. I considered that if the Major had been poisoned prior to coming to the village, as his brother had suggested, he would have already been displaying symptoms of it.

"No, he didn't," the doctor said. "Lady Caroline," he added, "perhaps it's best not to concern yourself with Eliot Yardley's speculations. It will not be in Lord Tatham's interest if people were to start whispering about the Major's death. After all, the man died in your uncle's library, and your uncle's interest in exotic plants is well known around these parts."

I bid the doctor a hurried goodbye and left the surgery perturbed. Had he given me a well-meaning caution, or had it been a warning?

CHAPTER 14

My meeting with the doctor had given me a lot to think about.

The Major had indeed been looking into Alice's death. It was possible that Alice had not taken her own life—the bruising could surely be a sign of foul play. Why had no one considered that possibility at the inquest following her drowning?

What had prompted the Major to look into the death in the first place? Had it been Alice's locket? What had been his theory? Had he reached any conclusions before his death? Had he shared his conclusions with anyone? Was he killed because he'd been getting too close to the truth?

Furthermore, the Major was most likely poisoned after arriving in the village, since when he'd gone to see the doctor, he had not been ill.

I also wondered if Dr. Perkins had been in love with Alice in his youth. Had the Major suspected as much? Was that why he'd gone to speak to the doctor first? And then, the most unlikely thought fluttered through my mind. Had the Major suspected Dr. Perkins of killing Alice? And had the doctor killed the Major to stop him from digging further?

I paused in my stride. What had occasioned this rather strange idea? Well, I reasoned with myself, the doctor was in possession of Uncle's poisons, he'd warned me to stop investigating, and he'd refused to consider that poisoning might have led to the Major's death. Were those not the actions of a guilty man? Circumstantially, then, Dr. Perkins had means and opportunity. And if he'd been in love with Alice, he might have had a motive. But surely the whole notion was foolish.

Resuming my walk down the village's main street, casually admiring the pretty tearooms, quaint shopfronts, and neat facades brightened with pots of flowers, I puzzled over perhaps the most intriguing element of my visit to Dr. Perkins —the book on Indian medicinal substances on the doctor's desk. Its subject matter was too topical to be accidental. Had the doctor been looking up the poison contained in the rosary pea? Did he actually believe Eliot Yardley's theory? Why, then, was he denying it?

Women smiled at me politely, some ruefully, and men doffed their hats as I passed. They all gave me slightly curious glances. No doubt they'd heard I was Lord Tatham's niece. Perhaps the doctor was right to be cautious, I conceded. One did not want to push the poisoned-Major theory too soon.

Uncle's penchant for deadly plants was bound to become conflated with the Major's death in the locals' minds.

I found myself in front of *The Fox and Hart*, the village inn. The doctor had warned me not to pry into the Major's death, but he'd said nothing about looking into Alice's. With that thought, I crossed the Inn's threshold.

It was only after entering and catching a glimpse of myself in a looking glass that I realized I was still wearing my makeup. I applied a handkerchief to wipe off the effect, but the friction only made my eyes and nose redder. I sighed. Perhaps it was for the best. It lent me a certain appearance of grief.

Alice's mother, Mrs. Harlan, upon realizing I was the niece of her landlord, was only too happy to invite me to her private quarters for tea. While she busied herself with the tea things, arranging them with the light touch of a practiced landlady, I regarded her, searching for evidence in her of her daughter's beauty.

She was a small woman with delicate features —a straight nose, a pleasant oval, a shapely mouth. But grief and age, she was no younger than sixty, had left their mark. The veiled eyes, hollow cheeks and deep frown lines spoke of sorrow unassuaged by time.

Yet, it was evident she took pride in both her appearance and her inn. Her white hair was pulled back into a bun, a neat apron covered a tidy dress, a crisp white tablecloth adorned the table, and a small posy in a tiny vase stood at its center.

The curiosity with which she surveyed me after taking her seat suggested that perhaps she hoped to learn as much from me as I from her. We spoke briefly of Uncle, Mrs. Harlan politely praising him as an excellent landlord. The topic of the Major's death could not be avoided for long, however, and etiquette dictated that it was I who had to broach it first. I cast about for a way to lead into it.

"It was quite a shock for Uncle Albert to find Major Yardley in his library," I said. "I wonder if the Major knew he was ill and returned to England to see his relations one last time."

"Poor man," Mrs. Harlan said. "I can't say that I had very warm feelings towards him, on account of my Alice, but the Major was very poorly the last few days. I wonder what made him leave his bed in the middle of the night and walk all the way to Lord Tatham's?" She looked at me expectantly.

"Perhaps he felt he didn't have long to live and wished to bid his brother farewell," I said with perfect innocence.

The landlady gave me a scrutinizing look. Perhaps she, like I, realized that, had a farewell been his purpose, the Major would have most likely gone to the Vicarage or the Dowager's House, both of which were situated closer to the Inn.

"I understand, however," I said quickly, to

stem any further speculation about the Major's motivation to seek a meeting with Uncle on the night of his death, "that the Major did not call for the doctor when he fell ill."

"Yes, that was strange," said Mrs. Harlan. "I offered to fetch the doctor, of course, but he refused. Said he felt better. Though I could see he looked worse. But men are stubborn. And the fewer dealings I have with the doctor the better. I wouldn't put it past him to accuse me of slipping something in the Major's food." She scowled. "Doesn't approve of some remedies I brew. I don't know why he objects. They are all natural."

The rosary pea was natural, I mused, but that didn't prevent it from being deadly. Though I did not share this observation.

"I think the doctor disapproves that the womenfolk still prefer to come to me with their troubles," she added.

I smiled guilelessly, as though politely not understanding her meaning.

"Major Yardley's return was a surprise to all," I said, making what I hoped was an innocuous enough statement to steer the conversation towards the true purpose of my visit.

Mrs. Harlan nodded. "No one was more surprised than me to see him at my door," she said with a note of derision. "You know, I've spent twenty years blaming him for my Alice's death."

Her turn of phrase caught my attention, but I

judged it wiser to ignore it for now. "It must have been so difficult for you," I said truthfully.

"It was. And at first, I meant to turn him away, but then curiosity got the better of me. What was he doing back here? Your Ladyship will probably laugh and think that I'm only saying this because I'm her mother, but I think he didn't return to see his family. Otherwise, why did he stay at the Inn and not with his brothers?" She shook her head. "No, he came back because he felt guilty about Alice."

There was that word again. "Guilty?" I asked.

Unlike the Vicar's wife, my question seemed to please Mrs. Harlan. She nodded. "You know he left my Alice and went to India when his father, the late Lord Tatham, would not allow the marriage?" I nodded. "And I've always been too polite to say it," she continued, "but in my mind, he as good as killed my little girl."

I inclined my head in sympathy. "Was her death not accidental?" I asked innocently after taking a sip of tea.

"That's what the coroner and the old doctor, Dr. Graham, said. But the bobby found her necklace by the lake, didn't he?"

I frowned. "What necklace?"

"Her locket. The one Richard, the Major, gave to her just before he left, as a promise to return."

I swallowed my surprise with another sip of tea. Was that the locket the Vicar's wife now wore?

"Alice wore it constantly after that," her mother continued. "I think she thought of it as an engagement ring, poor child." She shook her head. Then she looked at me. "Don't they say that suicides remove their spectacles?"

I nodded slowly.

"There, you see. Richard had gifted Alice a leather writing case. Well, it was little more than a leather folder with some paper, a place for a pencil, and some pockets on the inside of the flap. She'd taken it to the lake to write him a letter. Her farewell letter. The locket was inside one of the pockets. Alice had removed it before going into the water."

I nodded solemnly, but was quite perplexed. If the locket had been found by the lake, how did Margaret Yardley come to have it? But I couldn't ask that. Not yet. "Did the evidence of the locket and the letter come out during the inquest?" I asked instead.

Mrs. Harlan shook her head, and one corner of her mouth twisted somewhat bitterly. "The village bobby had a soft spot for me." She touched her face instinctively as though remembering her youth for a moment. "He brought the case to me, together with the letter she'd been writing. I asked him not to mention it. He agreed that there was no reason to muddle things. Kept them out of evidence. He was a good man. Turned a blind eye. If Alice's death was ruled a suicide, she could not be buried properly." She glanced at me as though to see if I'd understood. "He actually hadn't noticed the locket. Hadn't checked the pockets of the case. I found the locket later, but didn't say anything to the police."

"May I see the letter?" I said a bit too eagerly.

The landlady didn't seem put off by my forwardness. I knew from experience that people sometimes felt more at ease sharing their burdens with strangers. She left the parlor and soon came back with a slip of paper in her hand.

Mrs. Harlan watched me closely as I unfolded the note. Age had yellowed the paper, and the pencil writing was quite faint, but the sharp crease in the middle told me that the letter had been kept lovingly between the pages of a book. I looked for a moment at the hand; the loops executed with care, as if striving for perfection. Or was it the hand of a young woman who wished to appear elegant to a man above her station?

"Dear Richard," I read. "I fear this letter will reach you too late for you to do anything about it. And for that, I am truly sorry. Why did you have to leave? Life has become unbearable, for I can no longer ignore the spiteful rumors. I have thought about the promise you made me, but it is not enough. I have made my decision." I looked up from the letter. "It's unfinished."

Mrs. Harlan nodded. "I didn't want my little girl's letter being read out at the inquest," she said. She had not understood my meaning. "And if they'd read it out, they would have said that it was a suicide note. I couldn't have that." She shook her head and gazed into the distance. Pain flickered across her face, and her mouth tightened. "That's why I say the Major as good as killed her. It's clear from her note that she blamed him for leaving her behind to deal with all the vicious gossip. That's why she took her life."

I could see how Mrs. Harlan would think that this was a suicide note. But there was another explanation. To me, it was simply the letter of a young woman breaking off her understanding with her young man. But for some reason, she had not finished her letter. Had she been interrupted? By her assailant, perhaps?

"Did the Major see this note?" I asked.

She nodded. "At first, I didn't show it to him. But then he came back one afternoon with Alice's locket, wanting to know how the Vicar's wife had come to have it. It all came out then—Alice writing her letter on the shore, taking off her locket..."

I frowned, even more confused now. Hadn't Margaret Yardley been wearing it yesterday at dinner? "The Major had the locket?" I asked.

"Yes," Mrs. Harlan said. An emotion that I could not place broke through her voice. "I hated seeing it again. After Alice's death, I gave it to Margaret. Alice and her were good friends. Margaret was in such a bad state after Alice's death. Kept to her bed for days. Though, come to think of it, she was sick even before then. I remember, because Alice complained she had no one to talk to." Mrs. Harlan paused and gazed down at the table, unseeing. "After Margaret got better," she continued, after a moment, "she came to visit with me, to see how I was doing. I showed her the letter and locket. And she asked if she could keep the locket. I gave it to her most willingly. What did I want with a reminder of the man who abandoned Alice and drove her to her death?"

Thoughts began to swirl in my mind about Margaret Yardley's unhealthy attachment to that necklace.

"If Richard hadn't left, Alice would still be alive," Mrs. Harlan was saying, but I was only half-listening. "Villages are wicked places. The most vicious rumors began to spread after she drowned. That she'd taken her life because she was with child. Why didn't she speak to me about it? There are ways...but of course she wasn't...the doctor's examination would have shown something like that." She was speaking to herself now, lost in her memories. "And the thing is, it wasn't Alice who was with child that summer. Perhaps it was providence that took the Major's life. Balance has been restored."

All I could think of at that moment was the Vicar's wife. How was it, I wondered, that she had been wearing the necklace last night? Had the

Major given it back to her? Or had she taken it from him after his death?

I couldn't wait to take leave of Mrs. Harlan and find a way to speak to Margaret Yardley. Only later did I think that I should have asked who'd been with child that summer.

CHAPTER 15

I left Mrs. Harlan to her thoughts and memories, excusing myself by saying that I'd promised to lend a hand to Margaret Yardley with preparations for tomorrow's funeral. The fib brought on a momentary pang of guilt, but I told myself that finding out what had really happened to Alice was the best way I could help her mother.

I had not dared ask what Mrs. Harlan had really thought of the attachment between her daughter and Richard. She probably had encouraged it. But even now, with all the changes the war had brought to social norms, such a union would be frowned upon. Back then, it would have been unthinkable. My thoughts returned to the Major's motivation for leaving England. Was that the conduct of a man in love? Or had he left to extricate himself from an inconvenient association? Had he hoped that Alice, as admired as she'd been, would marry in his absence? But things had gone terribly wrong.

In my hurry to speak to the Vicar's wife, I had not thought to ask Mrs. Harlan if the Major had shared with her any theories he might have had about Alice's death. Upon reflection, however, I decided that had he mentioned any such musings, Mrs. Harlan would not still be under the impression that Alice had taken her own life.

I felt as though I was retracing the Major's steps. Like him, I now knew about the locket, the letter, and the doctor's report? To me, the clues suggested that, for some reason, Alice had decided to break off her understanding with Richard. That's why she'd taken off the necklace—to return it to him. She most likely planned to include it with the letter she'd been writing to him. But someone had interrupted her. Had the same person hit her on the head and then pushed her into the lake to drown?

What had the Major thought of these clues? Had he also suspected that Alice could have been murdered? If he had, he must have wondered not only why she'd been murdered, but by whom. Had he reached any conclusions? Had he been murdered to prevent him from sharing his theories with the police? So absorbed was I in my thoughts that it did not occur to me, even for a moment, that following the Major's footsteps might lead me to his fate.

While I could not speak to the Major—though my aunts would argue otherwise—I could at least try to get some answers from the Vicar's wife. Why had Margaret Yardley asked to keep the locket after

Alice's death? Why had she worn it for twenty years? Did others know that the locket had been a gift to Alice from Richard? And how, if the Major had had the locket in his possession before his death, had it found its way back to Margaret by yesterday evening?

As expected, Margaret Yardley was at the Vicarage. The Vicar might be responsible for tomorrow's service, but it fell on his wife to prepare to receive the mourners afterwards. A maid showed me to the drawing room, where her mistress was counting plates and linen napkins.

The Vicar's wife welcomed me most courteously. She assumed that I'd come to pay my respects to the Major and regretted to inform me that the body had been taken to the funeral parlor.

"That way, we can have a longer procession to the church tomorrow morning," she said.

The arrangement suited me. I preferred not to look at the body.

Margaret Yardley had shed her pallid countenance of the previous night and had regained some color in her cheeks. Her eyes were bright enough and friendly. While I observed all this, however, I did not fail to notice that today she wore a dress that left her neck exposed. I frowned —there was no locket. I fought the urge to ask about it immediately.

I took the seat offered, declined tea, and instead suggested I could help with the preparations.

Margaret Yardley blushed at the suggestion and looked down at the linen in her hands. "Mary is run off her feet helping Cook with tomorrow's reception," she said as though apologizing for doing work.

I nodded in understanding. "Are you expecting many guests after the funeral?" I asked.

"Many will be curious to attend," she said.

The implication that the guests would consist mostly of the village gossips was not lost on me. But instead, I said, "Yes, I suppose the Major's old acquaintances would wish to pay their respects." Though I wondered how many of his contemporaries from the village had died in the war.

"Richard was always better friends with his brothers than anyone else. There were few young men in the area with whom he could associate. And he didn't have the aptitude for University. I suppose that's why he ended up in the Army. He had a small circle of friends."

"Like Dr. Perkins," I said.

"Dr. Perkins?" Margaret Yardley asked, slightly surprised. "Yes, Richard was friends with John. Though John was mostly up at University by then. But I suppose he must have come down often enough, especially during the summer holidays."

"And you were part of that circle, I believe," I said.

She nodded. "Bernard was courting me, and

Richard was courting Alice." She paused as though to let the memories float up in her mind. "Despite everything that came after...Richard and Alice...that summer is imprinted on my mind as having been a happy one. Filled with love and sunshine, and a warm breeze. I remember light filtering through the leaves, dappling the surface of the lake. Our boats gliding over the surface of the water as the men guided them. There were picnics on the bank, in the tall grass. Laughter, happiness. The heady confidence of youth. It had a magical quality."

Margaret Yardley stayed with her remembrances for a while. There was a lovely serenity in her features.

"Quite the change from short pants and peashooters," I added with a smile.

She laughed. "The boys had outgrown those things by then; we were young adults. The future in front of us. Richard was twenty years old. And Alice, Bernard and I right behind him at nineteen."

"And what about Eliot?" I asked. "Was he not part of your circle?"

"Yes, there was Eliot, as well. Always spoiling things." She laughed again. "He was three years younger than Richard. Those differences matter when you are young. I suppose Richard didn't wish to associate with a boy of seventeen. But Eliot didn't see it that way. He was always his brother's shadow. Richard would get annoyed with him for always lurking about. They had some heated arguments about it." She was silent for a moment, lost in her recollections. "Though, looking back at it now, I suppose there was some rivalry between the two of them. Their father saw to that. He liked rivalries. Eliot was always competing with Richard, wanting what he had."

"Two young brothers courting two beautiful women," I said. Margaret Yardley blushed. "It must have been difficult for Eliot to be the odd one out," I added.

"Yes, I suppose. Though now that I think about it, there was always Julia. She was in love with Eliot. We could all see it. And I suppose he returned her attentions. Perhaps for old-time's sake, when they played as children on the estate."

"Was Julia not part of the group?" I asked, surprised. The previous night's dinner conversation had left me with the impression that Julia had been a closer friend to the brothers than Margaret.

"Julia was younger than us, and hadn't made her way into the grown-up circle," Margaret Yardley said. I had the feeling that she took some pleasure in the fact. "She was for a long time what one would now term a tomboy. Always parading around with bruises and scraped knees, short dresses with stains on them, running after Eliot. I suppose she caught him in the end." She smiled at her own witticism. "How things change. She was a pudgy little thing, and then she went away and came back tall and quite pretty, I suppose." She tucked a stray hair behind her ear. "Eliot was certainly smitten enough with her to propose to her."

"Perhaps he aspired to be like Richard," I quipped. "Always wanting what his brother had."

"What?" Margaret Yardley asked sharply.

For a moment I was taken aback by her reaction. "I meant that perhaps Eliot wanted to be engaged because Richard was engaged to Alice."

"Oh, yes. I see," she said. "Though, I don't think there was any formal engagement between Richard and Alice. He was certainly in love with her. But I don't believe it ever came to anything formal that she could reproach him with."

"But the locket he gave her," I said. "Didn't he give it to her as a promise to return and marry her?"

Margaret Yardley touched the place on her breast where the locket would have rested. She seemed surprised not to find it there. I observed the confused emotion that flickered across her face for a moment.

"You're not wearing your necklace today," I said, perhaps a bit reckless.

"Richard asked for it back," she said quietly, a flush creeping up her neck. "When he came to the village, we ran into each other on the grounds of Albert's estate. He confronted me about it. Wanted to know how I came to have it. And demanded it back." She was silent for a moment, then looked up at me. "The locket was not on him," she said.

I cocked my head in incomprehension.

"When I laid him out. It was not on him," she said. "And it wasn't among his things. Mrs. Harlan gave me his possessions back."

"Why is the locket so important?" I asked.

She gazed at her hands. "I guess it isn't," she said. "Richard's leaving changed Alice," she added after a moment.

"In what way?" I asked, surprised both by the assertion and the change of topic.

"It hardened her. I think she realized that she could use her beauty to get what she wanted. Perhaps she'd always done that, and it was only I who came to realize it then," she added pensively. "She'd set her sights on the most eligible young man in the village, and when that man was denied to her, she turned her attention to someone else."

"Who was the man she turned her attention to?" I asked.

"She did not confide in me, but she hinted, after Richard left, that she didn't have to wait for him if she didn't wish to. Boasted about it, even. I think she delighted in having so many suitors. It happened so suddenly, the way she changed her mind about Richard."

I regarded Margaret Yardley for a moment. Had she been jealous of Alice's many suitors? Had she been obsessed with Alice's beauty? Was that why she'd kept her locket all those years? And then another thought occurred to me. Was it possible that Alice had set her sights on Bernard as the next most eligible young man in the village? I suppressed a snigger. Alice with her many suitors would surely not have settled for being a missionary's wife.

Thoughts of a mysterious man in the background began swirling in my mind. Hiding, watching, biding his time, waiting for his opportunity, taking it when Richard had left. Why had Alice died?

"How did Richard learn about Alice's death?" I asked.

"Bernard wrote to him," Margaret Yardley said. "I suppose he convinced Richard not to return. Told him to build a new life away from all that was no longer here for him. My husband has always possessed the gift of helping people through their troubles. I suppose that is what makes him a good Vicar and a good sermon writer. And an excellent correspondent. Much good that has done us," she added with some bitterness. She was twisting one of the napkins in her lap.

I looked at her quizzically. "I don't understand."

She laughed bitterly. "You must have been the only one at dinner yesterday who failed to notice Eliot's insinuations that we'd poisoned Richard."

I gasped. "That's not the impression I got at

all," I protested, convincingly I hoped. "As far as I understood, your brother-in-law was only referring to the poison used on cattle in the Bengal."

Margaret Yardley shifted in her seat as though it had suddenly grown uncomfortable.

"Oh, Margaret," the Vicar's voice came from the door, startling us both. "Why do you always have to be so guarded about it?" Exasperation broke through his voice. "It's no use being so secretive. That's why people gossip. You've done nothing wrong. And at any rate, I daresay everyone already knows about it."

"Writing to Eliot was a mistake," she said without looking at her husband.

He crossed the room with determination and sat in a chair opposite me. With his hands on his knees, he looked earnestly at me and said, "While we were in India, there was an incident. Not a murder, as Eliot suggested last night. Just a mix-up."

A whimper escaped from Margaret Yardley. The Vicar and I both turned to look at her. She had gone quite pale again.

"No one is blaming you, my dear." He then turned to me. "There was so much poison in India. Poisonous plants everywhere, yes, but also in the house, various noxious preparations for killing vermin and insects, or keeping mold at bay. There was a confusion about two kettles in the kitchen.

One contained a brew made ready to deal with an infestation in the house. It was the one that ended up being used to make tea. The servants should have warned Margaret. We wrote to Eliot for legal advice. Fortunately, no one died, and all recovered." He looked away and sat silently for a while. "It is just like Eliot to see evil where there is none. Take the rosary pea he mentioned last night. As the name might suggest, the seeds are rarely used for poison. Bright red, they resemble ladybirds, and the natives most often employ them in the making of *malas*, rosaries. Even the Indian deities Vishnu and Krishna are depicted wearing necklaces made from the seeds."

As the clock struck the noon hour, the Vicar and his wife invited me to join them for lunch. But I declined. I had much to consider. Plus, I doubted that in her husband's presence, I could learn more from Margaret about her meeting with the Major, the locket, or Alice's death.

CHAPTER 16

As I drove back to Uncle's estate, I once again considered the locket. What was its significance?

Why was it missing? And if Margaret Yardley or the Major didn't have it, where was it? I was convinced that the locket held a clue to Alice's death. And the Major's. I was growing certain that the killer had taken it. If I could find the locket, I would find the killer.

There was only one lake on Uncle's estate, and on the way back, I stopped by its shore. The calm surface sparkled in the noon sunshine. The trees of the parkland reached almost to the water's edge, where tall grasses, reeds and sedges overtook them, covering the bank and spilling into the water. Near me, a willow swept its delicate branches along the water's surface. As I followed the light ripples, I could see in my mind's eye boats gliding quietly across the lake, just as Margaret had described.

But the one thing I could not see was rocks. I didn't know exactly where Alice had gone into the water, but if the lakeside looked much like it did today, most of the bank would have been overgrown and inaccessible. Where I stood was the only place one could walk down to the water. Somewhere along here, under the shade of a tree perhaps, must be where Alice had been writing her letter. This must be where she'd gone into the water. And there were no rocks unless some were hiding under the surface. How could Alice have hit her head going in? Why had no one considered that?

I got back into my car and continued towards the Hall.

It seemed as though at the time of Alice's death, people had rushed to hush up a scandal. The specter of a suicide had been so disagreeable that a verdict of accidental death had been pushed through with the help of the constable. Otherwise, how could one explain that obvious details had been overlooked? Why had no one noted the absence of rocks by the lakeside? And why had no one raised the most obvious question: if Alice had been writing a farewell letter, why had she not signed it? Several people had seen the letter —the constable, Alice's mother, even Margaret. What had prevented them from seeing the truth? I wondered if there had been something in Alice's behavior in the days leading up to her death that had made the people closest to her believe that she could indeed have taken her life? In the letter they found by the water, they saw what they'd expected.

But I could review the details of Alice's death with the detachment time affords. And I saw foul play. Had the Major also seen that? I was convinced that he had, and that the Major had been killed by Alice's killer.

I could therefore eliminate Alice's mother from my list of suspects. Although she had the skills to poison the Major, had plenty of opportunity to do so while he was staying at the Inn, and blamed the Major for her daughter's death, I doubted she'd killed her own daughter. And if the break-ins were connected to the Major's death, Alice's mother had no motive to steal Uncle's imprecise distillates, or rummage through a curio cabinet for a bracelet.

What I had learned this morning—the crowd of young men in love with Alice, according to Dr. Perkins, and Alice's lover, according to Margaret—led me to suspect that a love triangle lay at the heart of this mystery. Either of the Major's brothers could have been Alice's mysterious lover. After Richard's departure, they were the area's two most eligible bachelors.

A jealous lover could have killed Alice in a fit of rage. But why would her lover kill her after Richard had left? Had she rejected him? Had she refused his advances, determined to wait for the Major? But Margaret, and Alice's own letter, suggested otherwise. Alice was breaking off her understanding with the Major.

So what could have happened to lead to her death?

And then, as these things happen, a rather unpleasant idea materialized. Could the Major's father have been part of this love triangle? A shudder crept over me. Yet, such things happened. Men of wealth, especially in their old age, had a preference for beautiful young women. In the case of the late Lord Tatham, there was even a precedent. For his second wife, he had chosen a young woman of low birth.

But even if the late Lord Tatham was the mysterious lover, was it likely that he would have killed Alice? It seemed to me that she would have enjoyed being mistress of the house, even if it was only for a short while.

But perhaps he'd killed her because she was the reason his favorite son had gone away. He'd opposed the marriage and perhaps blamed Alice for Richard's flight to India. Had his anger overtaken him, killing Alice in a moment of madness?

The Major's stay at the Inn, rather than with his family, suggested that he might have blamed them for Alice's death. Had the Major been killed to protect the memory of the father? Yet, none of the sons showed much love for their father. Were they likely to kill to preserve his memory? I decided that this was unlikely.

Of course, the death of Alice and the Major need

not be connected. The Major could have been killed for his money. His brothers would most likely inherit the Major's annuity. Furthermore, both brothers were familiar with the rosary pea. Had Eliot Yardley's unexpected claim that the Major had been poisoned been some sort of bluff, serving to remove suspicion from himself and implicate the Vicar at the same time? And since the brothers had grown up on the estate, both had intimate knowledge of the secret greenhouse and the curio cabinet, making it quite plausible that either of them could have broken in.

Then, a rather different thought took shape. Uncle Albert was getting on in age. His stepbrothers were next in line to inherit the title and estate. Twenty years younger, they would have plenty of time to enjoy the privileges of the peerage. With the Major out of the way, the Vicar was next in line. But if Eliot Yardley could implicate the Vicar in the Major's death, and the Vicar was found guilty, he would inherit the title next. Could he be so devious? I conceded that as a barrister he had the knowledge to twist evidence to gain a conviction. I shuddered at the unpleasant thought.

I had to admit, however, that killing one brother and framing another so that a third brother would inherit was a rather dubious way to go about gaining a title. It was imprecise and messy, leaving far too many things to chance. I pushed the notion out of my mind.

What about the brothers' wives? Could one of them be the killer? I could not quite make out Julia Yardley's motive for killing either Alice or the Major. She'd been younger than the rest and out of their circle. Unless, I considered, Alice's secret lover had been Eliot Yardley, and Julia had killed Alice out of jealousy. But Julia had been away the summer Richard had left. Though, upon reflection, Julia did strike me as an ambitious person. Perhaps she lent her husband a hand in framing the Vicar so that Eliot Yardley could inherit Uncle's title in the end. I chuckled at the improbability.

The answer to this mystery most likely lay in the events of that golden summer that Margaret Yardley remembered so fondly.

I sighed as I thought of the Vicar's wife. Her attachment to Alice's locket was rather peculiar. Why had she searched the Major's body and among his possessions for it? Why did she want it back? Why had she worn it for twenty years?

Had she been trying to throw me off the scent, as it were, by saying that she didn't have the locket? She could have taken it from the Major's body after his death, and no one would have known. And what about the incident in India? Her husband had been too quick to explain it away. What if Margaret had a penchant for poisoning her enemies?

I smirked. Since my gloves had served me so well at the doctor's, I had also left them behind at the Vicarage. Prior to driving back to Uncle's, I'd gone back to retrieve them. Returning to the house via the garden path, I'd inadvertently overheard an argument between the Vicar and his wife through the open French doors. His tone had been low but insistent. He was demanding to know what was going on. There were too many poisonings for his liking. He said that he'd always believed the matter in India to have been an accident, but if the Major really was poisoned, could he continue to believe that Margaret was innocent?

It was a rather suggestive conversation.

Turning onto Uncle's drive and proceeding up the tree-lined avenue, I reviewed my last two suspects. If the Major's death was connected to events from that fateful summer twenty years ago, and to a love triangle, then Dr. Perkins had to be on my list. I was convinced he'd been in love with Alice. The reason why he would kill her, I admit, was at the moment a little murky. But if he had, and the Major had discovered some evidence against the doctor, then that gave him a motive. The doctor also had a book about Indian poisons on his desk. Plus, the way he denied the possibility that the Major could have been poisoned was rather suspicious. Yet, the doctor had been away at the time of Alice's death.

Finally, as I drew up to the Hall, and the stable

boy ran across the gravel sweep to attend to the car, I thought about Mr. Graves. I could not connect him to Alice in any way. But perhaps the death of Alice had nothing to do with the Major's death. Perhaps I'd been looking at this all wrong. Perhaps the Major's death was connected to some family treasure, and the answer was to be found in the library.

As Wilford greeted me, however, it transpired that Mr. Graves might soon be permanently eliminated as a suspect.

"If you are willing to delay your lunch for a few minutes, my lady," Wilford said, "I think you should follow me to Mr. Graves' bedroom."

I looked at him quizzically, but his face was inscrutable.

"Mr. Graves believes he was attacked near the greenhouse this morning," Wilford said as he led me up the stairs.

"Attacked! How?!"

"I believe he'd prefer to tell you himself."

We hurried down the corridor towards Mr. Graves' bedroom, and once Wilford's knock was answered by a weak voice, we went in.

Inside, the room and its occupant were not as expected. The curtains were open, light streamed through, and the victim was sitting up in his bed, propped up by plump white pillows. The gravity of Wilford's voice had led me to believe that Mr. Graves was on his deathbed. But instead of a priest, it was Dr. Perkins and Uncle who were sitting by his bedside.

The look Mr. Graves wore suggested that he quite enjoyed the attention he was receiving. An appreciative smile flickered across his face when I entered. For a man who had been hiding in the shadows for the last day or so, it was unexpected. But perhaps he was one of those people who relished being tended to when ill, I mused.

Mr. Graves truly was a near-copy of Uncle Albert. Even his hair crackled cheerfully around his head in the manner of Uncle's, when he had a secret to share. His sparkling eyes also betrayed his excitement.

Refraining from asking what he'd been doing around Uncle's greenhouse, I asked him to tell me more about the attack instead.

"Well," Mr. Graves began, "there is very little to tell. It all happened so suddenly. As I was walking, taking the fresh morning air, a wasp buzzed by me. I have a dreadful fear of being stung, and quickly...ducked to the ground." He threw me a furtive glance upon this divulgence.

I frowned. I failed to see how this was an attack, and why the doctor and Uncle were gathered round Mr. Graves.

"But you were not stung?" I said. Judging by his rosy cheeks and bright eyes, Mr. Graves was not ill. Or in any pain.

"No, that was the lucky thing. It was as though

Providence had intervened. At the very moment the wasp passed by my ear, I tripped." He gave me a meaningful look. "I believe if I hadn't lost my step, I would have been stung directly in the neck."

I wanted to counter that wasps were not projectiles, but seeing the rather somber expression on Dr. Perkins' face, I judged that it was wiser to withhold my objection.

"I remained in the prone position for some time, waiting for the danger to pass," he continued. "After my heartbeat had slowed down, and I'd regained some of my composure, I proceeded to examine my situation. I strained to hear if the wasp was still in my vicinity, but could hear no buzzing. However, I am a thorough man. It would not be the first time that an insect tangled itself up in my hair." Uncle gave a sympathetic nod. "So, I ran a cautious hand, just to be sure that the creature was still not hiding on my person. And that was when I found this."

Mr. Greaves reached towards a small glass vial, similar to the ones Uncle carried in his pockets. He picked it up gingerly between two fingers and rattled it. The item inside clinked against the glass sides, as though a small pebble.

I peered closer. The object indeed looked like a small whitish stone. But there was something strange about it. Its shape was too geometrical, as though the stone had been fashioned into an acute triangle.

"What is it?" I asked.

"If the *Pharmacographia Indica* can be trusted," Dr. Perkins said, "we are looking at a deadly weapon. A sharp point made of the pulp of the rosary pea."

CHAPTER 17

"How can you be sure?!" I exclaimed rather louder than I had intended, but so many emotions and ideas in my head were suddenly vying for attention. Was this how the Major was killed? Why was Mr. Graves attacked? And how exactly was he attacked?

"Well, I have no definitive proof," the doctor hedged. "Short of administering it to someone, I cannot be certain. There are no tests for abrin—that's the poisonous substance inside the rosary pea. But this arrowhead, for lack of a better description, looks precisely like what's described in the book. According to the description, the seeds are cracked, the soft pulp inside ground down to a smooth paste with a bit of water, then shaped into a cone and left to dry in the sun. Once dry, it becomes quite hard, and the point can be sharpened further."

"How long does the process take?" I asked.

"No more than a day," the doctor answered.

"And all of this was described in your book?" I

asked, astonished. It was like a murderer's manual.

He nodded. "I believe the information in my book was borrowed from the meticulous descriptions of rosary pea poisonings supplied by the Bengal Superintendent of Police."

I gasped. This was the book Eliot Yardley had read, and that Uncle also had in his library. "And how is this arrowhead then used to kill someone?"

"It's attached to the end of a stick and then driven under the skin with a sharp blow."

"But wouldn't the victim remove the cone immediately?" I asked.

The doctor shook his head. "Apparently, even if one does try to remove it, a piece is inevitably left under the skin. Even the smallest amount causes the victim to die in about three days." He glanced at Mr. Graves, who'd gone rather pale. "Mr. Graves is quite lucky that the arrow point missed him."

I turned to look at Uncle's cousin, who was slowly sinking into his pillow, perspiration beading on his forehead. "But Mr. Graves," I said, "no one attacked you, correct? I mean, no one came at you with a stick."

The man shook his head feebly.

"Then someone must have shot the point at him," I said, turning to the doctor. He nodded. "But that must be how the Major was poisoned as well. From a distance. Otherwise, he would have recognized his attacker immediately and alerted someone. Now you have proof that the Major did not die of a heart attack."

The doctor looked at me and sighed heavily. "I have no proof that this is how the Major was poisoned, or indeed that he was poisoned at all."

"But we have the poisonous arrowhead!" I objected, gesturing to the glass vial. "And the cut behind his ear!" I exclaimed, remembering.

"Yes, I agree that it's all highly suggestive. But," he said, forestalling me, "I have absolutely no evidence when it comes to Richard's death. It's all wild supposition. We would not even be talking about this if Eliot Yardley had not turned our minds towards this method of killing." He shook his head. "The coroner is a fastidious man. I'd be risking my career if I went to him with the little we have. I'll be laughed out of his office. I've looked it up—by the time the victim dies, abrin is long gone from the microscopic wound where the tip of the arrowhead entered the body. I have nothing," he added, his tone suggesting that he truly was sorry he could not do more.

"So short of finding someone with the poisonous point embedded in their neck, and the killer standing over them, we have nothing," I said scornfully.

The doctor smiled politely. "And even then, the evidence would only be sufficient to convict the killer of the death of that unlucky soul, not of the Major's." He sighed again. "Lady Caroline, unfortunately, abrin is a rather clever poison.

Modern science has not yet devised a way to detect it."

I nodded dejectedly.

Perhaps touched by my disappointment, the doctor continued, his tone softened, "If we at least had the weapon. Or the seeds. Then, maybe the coroner would consider looking further into the case."

I nodded again.

"Well," the doctor said after a few moments, "I've done what I came to do. Mr. Graves looks unharmed, and the arrow point looks intact. The ordeal left him a bit shaken, and his blood pressure was rather low when I arrived. But I think he's recovering nicely. There is nothing else for me to do here." He got up to leave.

"But what if the killer attacks Mr. Graves again?" I said.

By the squeak that escaped Mr. Graves, it was clear that he had not considered the possibility.

The doctor surveyed the man on the bed, whose pallid countenance suggested that his blood pressure was dropping rapidly again. "Mr. Graves is free to call the police, of course," said the doctor. "But are you prepared for the investigation and the Press," he said, turning to me and regarding me over his glasses.

It was my turn to sigh. My mother's horrified face floated up in front of my eyes. She had sent me here in the hopes of keeping the Press away.

I nodded my acquiescence to the doctor. Considering the matter closed, Dr. Perkins gathered his Gladstone bag and left.

I waited until the door had closed behind the doctor and turned to Mr. Graves. "Did you see your assailant?" I asked.

"No," the man said with a shaky voice.

"Can you think of a reason why anyone would want to attack you?" I pressed.

This revitalized the man a bit, and he pulled himself up into a more upright position. "I am a scholar, Lady Caroline. I detest drawing-room dramas. I have tried to avoid becoming involved in the family's affairs, as they are so wholly unconnected with me."

With a small inclination of the head, I acknowledged his endeavor to appear morally upstanding.

"But during my stay," he continued, "I have been exposed to these affairs against my will."

I gave a nod that I hoped conveyed both understanding and sympathy. "Have you witnessed something that could have left you exposed to this attack?" I asked.

He contemplated for a moment. "I have. I saw the Major arguing with a woman on the edge of the woods a few days before he died."

"Who was the woman?"

"I couldn't say. She was wearing a wide-brimmed sun hat," he said.

I considered that Margaret Yardley's build was quite different from that of Julia Yardley, but perhaps Mr. Graves was not an observant man when it came to women. And anyway, the information was not very useful. Margaret Yardley had already told me of her meeting with the Major in the park.

"And you think you were attacked because you witnessed this meeting?" I asked. "Did either the woman or the Major see you?"

"I don't think so," he said slowly.

"And have you confronted either Margaret or Julia Yardley about what you observed?"

He shook his head. "Why would I? As I said, I've tried to stay out of the family's dealings."

"So it is unlikely that you were attacked because of what you witnessed," I said.

"I suppose," he said, sounding somewhat disappointed.

I regarded Mr. Graves for a moment. He considered himself an intelligent man. And he'd been here, observing the family, ever since the Major had returned. "Do you have theories of your own regarding the Major's death?" I asked.

He once again shook his head unhelpfully. I remembered the gaze he had leveled at someone in the drawing room after dinner last night. Could Mr. Graves be saying less than he knew? He wouldn't be foolish enough to try to blackmail a killer, would he?

"Could the attack on you be related to your research here?" I asked.

"Oh, no," he objected vehemently. "My research is purely scholarly."

"You haven't perhaps uncovered dark secrets in the archives?"

He smirked. "Nothing more than the usual intrigues and machinations of any noble family."

"Nothing that would suggest that the title should go to the cadet branch, perhaps?" I asked in jest.

"Alas, no."

Just then, a snore emanated from Uncle Albert, who'd dozed off in his chair. I turned from Mr. Graves to Uncle and back to Mr. Graves.

"Incidentally, where on the grounds did the attack take place today? By the greenhouse?" I asked.

Mr. Graves shifted in his supportive pillows and threw a furtive glance at me. "Yes, by the small greenhouse. I merely happened to be passing," he said rather defensively.

I smiled at him. I thought he was not entirely truthful. What had he been doing near the small greenhouse? Had he been snooping? Had it been mere curiosity or something else? The under-gardener, at least, had thought his behavior strange enough to warrant issuing a warning to

Uncle about it.

But that was not the reason I'd asked where the incident had taken place. I'd wondered if Uncle Albert had not been the intended target. My mind had jumped to the noise I'd heard the previous night, when Uncle and I had been ascending the stairs. I'd wondered then if someone had been hiding in the shadows. Had it been the killer? Had the killer tried to attack Uncle Albert today because of what he or she suspected the Major had told Uncle?

I turned my attention back to Mr. Graves. "What do you intend to do now?"

"I hadn't really considered what I should do next," he said.

"If someone is after you, it might be wiser to leave the estate," I suggested.

"But I haven't concluded my research," he objected.

I nodded. Perhaps Mr. Graves also didn't think he was the killer's intended target. He was gazing at Uncle Albert rather peculiarly.

"Do you intend to call the police?" I asked.

He brought his attention back to me with a snap. "Why?"

I gestured towards the vial containing the poisonous pellet.

"I don't see why I should," he said. "As the doctor said, it proves nothing."

I nodded in agreement. Who wanted the plodding police underfoot, anyway? A plan was hatching in my mind.

"But it will make a rather good story to tell at dinner parties," Mr. Graves added.

I smiled and congratulated him on enduring his ordeal with such good humor, but privately wondered if Mr. Graves got invited to many parties. Perhaps once this adventure became attached to his name, he would make a more compelling dinner-guest prospect.

"I do think it is rather advisable that you lie low, as it were, for a few days," I said, returning to the matter at hand. "It's perhaps best for the person who attacked you to think that they've hit their target."

He agreed that it was the most sensible course of action. After all, as he said, no one would expect him to be at the Major's funeral.

I gestured to Wilford that it was time to rouse Uncle and make our way to lunch. A lunch tray was arranged for Mr. Graves.

"Incidentally, Wilford, why are you set against Mr. Graves?" I asked as we made our way to the Dining Room.

Wilford looked as though he was about to object. "I am certain he is here for something to pilfer," he replied.

I smiled. Even the infallible Wilford was susceptible to unwarranted prejudices.

I waited until we were seated before resuming my musings. "Another thing intrigues me about the attack on Mr. Graves. Where did the attacker get the rosary peas to make the poisonous pellet?"

"Not from my plant," Uncle Albert piped up.

I nodded appeasingly. "But the question remains. Is it possible that the plant is growing on the estate somewhere?"

Uncle gave the matter some consideration. "No," he said categorically. "Much too cold for the blighter."

"But what if I do a survey of the estate? Could you draw a map for me of the path of poisonous plants?"

"I can show you," Uncle said, sounding rather excited by the prospect.

"No, I think it is more prudent for you to remain in the house, like Mr. Graves."

Uncle bristled. "Why should I?"

"We can't be certain the attacker didn't mean that poisonous dart for you, Uncle," I said gently. "It is possible that the assailant mistook Mr. Graves for you."

By the wrinkling of his nose, I could see that the suggestion was not to Uncle's liking. I wondered if that was because he realized his life was now in danger or because he didn't like being compared to his cousin. "Until the killer is caught, I think it is wiser to pretend that you are also ill. You need to remain inside the house. Even tomorrow."

"It would be unseemly for me to miss Richard's funeral!" he objected.

"I understand," I said. "But is it not better that you stay alive rather than worry about what people would say? If the killer sees you, they will know they have failed. And they will try again."

The way Uncle attacked his soup told me that death would be preferable to ruining one's reputation. I glanced at Wilford. I hoped he could prevail upon the old relation to see reason.

I made an additional decision during lunch—that the police had to be called in.

"Not to look into the matter of the Major's death or the attack on Mr. Graves," I said. "I concede that perhaps we don't have enough evidence for the police to pursue these. But we could ask the police to look into the break-ins. The killer, of course, need not know that. All we have to do is create the illusion that Uncle is dying—"

"I say!" he objected.

"—and that the police are here to investigate. It might spur the killer into action."

"Are you hoping for another attack, my lady?" asked Wilford dryly. His astonishment at my suggestion must have been great to allow himself to speak while he was serving a potato.

I let out a frustrated breath. I hadn't actually considered that. "Of course I'm not hoping for another attack. I'm hoping that it might prompt the killer to dispose of the murder weapon."

CHAPTER 18

The next morning, Wilford and I could be found sneaking across Uncle's estate on a secret mission. I'd sent a note to the Vicarage, excusing myself from attending the Major's funeral, on account of Uncle not feeling well due to some vague ailment. Uncle had at last been prevailed upon to go along with my plan, but not before many lively protestations.

I'd made no mention to Uncle's relations of the previous day's attack. I hoped the doctor had been as discreet as usual.

Thus, with Uncle sequestered in the house, the rest of the family at the funeral, and the local constable plodding around the Hall—the maids were instructed to serve him plenty of tea and cakes after he'd finished investigating the curio cabinet incident—Wilford and I were free to set my plan into motion.

"Have you considered, my lady," Wilford said as we crossed the park at a brisk pace, "Mr. Graves' reliability?"

I suppressed a smile and decided to play along. "What do you mean, Wilford?"

"How likely is it that his story is a true representation of events?" he continued. "I believe the veracity of his account falls apart under scrutiny."

"How so?"

"Well, it is possible that Mr. Graves prepared the poisonous pellet himself."

I nodded. I'd considered the possibility and ruled against it. "If we accept that to be true, then we must believe that it was Mr. Graves who killed the Major," I said. "And since the Major arrived in the village after Mr. Graves was already here, then it means that Mr. Graves must have known in advance that the Major would come to the village, and planned the whole thing ahead of time. But I don't believe that to be the case. There is something very rushed, very haphazard about all of these incidents." I was thinking of the break-ins, the Major's note to Uncle, and the attack on Mr. Graves. "The whole affair does not appear premeditated."

"Mr. Graves need not have planned it all in advance, my lady," Wilford objected. "Meeting the Major at Lord Tatham's estate could have been quite unexpected for both men. And then, Mr. Graves could have prepared the poisonous pellet in the same way as any of your other suspects."

I'd failed to consider that scenario. I'd always

thought that if the Major and Mr. Graves had known each other, their meeting here had been pre-arranged. "You mean we've left Uncle Albert alone with the killer?" I asked in mock shock. I didn't truly believe Mr. Graves to be a murderer. A pang of doubt cut through me for a moment, nevertheless. "We have nothing that connects him with the Major's death, except for their mutual interest in the library," I continued. "And why insert himself so centrally into the mystery, when most of the time no one even notices him?"

Wilford nodded. "The ability to appear unobtrusive is the mark of a skilled criminal."

I laughed. "But we will get nowhere with our theories if we don't solve the conundrum of how the killer got a hold of the rosary pea seeds to begin with," I said.

"Indeed, my lady," said Wilford.

"Despite Uncle's objections, the plant must grow somewhere on the estate," I insisted. To that end, I'd left instructions with the head gardener for his under-gardeners to scour the estate and collect cuttings of any plant with red berries. Then, I planned to ask Uncle Albert to inspect them all for the poisonous culprit.

That, however, was a job for this afternoon. At present, Wilford and I were headed to the Dowager's House, where Eliot Yardley lived with his wife. When we arrived, Wilford went round the back to the kitchen, to visit with the barrister's cook and parlormaid, as per our plan. While he kept them thus occupied, I used the front door to gain entrance and spy around the rest of the house. I was in search of any evidence, such as the missing locket, rosary pea seeds, poisonous pellets, or any device that might be used to shoot a pellet, such as a slingshot or a blowpipe, that might tie the barrister or his wife to the Major's death.

The Dowager's House, an English Baroque confection, was rather sumptuously decorated, making my job somewhat difficult. But I had attended Frau Baumgartnerhoff's finishing school in Switzerland, and while I had acquired few other skills, I had learned how to find things people wanted to hide. Frau Baumgartnerhoff believed that a proficiency in ferreting secrets out was the key to matrimonial happiness. She had been determined that not one of her charges should ever experience the bitter mortification of being the last to discover that her husband was having an affair. To that end, we'd all graduated with competencies that would make the Artful Dodger envious. Yet, though I searched thoroughly, and employed all of Frau Baumgartnerhoff's little insights into human psychology and folly, I could not find anything incriminating.

Exiting the house stealthily, and going round the back to collect Wilford from the kitchen, we made our way to the Vicarage. Once there, we repeated our ritual from earlier—I headed for the front door, while Wilford proceeded to the back. My strategy for investigating the Vicarage, however, was rather different. I never expected to find it devoid of people. Instead, I planned to use all the guests milling around after the funeral as a cover. I hoped no one would notice if I snuck about a few rooms. I could always claim to be in search of the lavatory.

As expected, upon entering the Vicarage, I found the funeral attendees had already gathered in the house for refreshments. The parlor was quite crammed with guests, and everyone was rather busy balancing a plate in one hand and a glass in another to notice as I made my way towards the stairs leading to the upper floor and bedrooms.

The Vicar's residence was decidedly easier to search. Bernard Yardley and his wife appeared to lead a much simpler life and had fewer possessions than the barrister. Nowhere was this more evident than in Margaret Yardley's jewelry box. I searched it in the hopes that the elusive locket had reappeared, but all it contained were trifles that could have come from an Indian bazaar. Once again, I failed to find anything incriminating.

I mumbled something about a lavatory to the women I met at the bottom of the stairs as I came down. While I felt disappointed not to have discovered anything, I'd gone into this plan knowing it was a long shot. I hesitated for a moment about how to proceed.

Then, I noticed Mrs. Harlan making her way back to the kitchen with an empty tray. She was obviously lending a hand at the reception. I followed her to the kitchen. Wilford was sitting with Cook out of earshot, engrossed in some sort of gossip. I waited for the maid to leave the kitchen with a tray before approaching Mrs. Harlan. Something had been bothering me since we'd spoken the previous day.

"Mrs. Harlan," I said, keeping my voice low and my back to Cook. "Yesterday, you said that you knew someone had been with child the summer Alice died. Who was it?"

Mrs. Harlan finished arranging the egg-and-cress sandwiches on a plate before turning to look at me. "Oh, maybe it was just my fancy. It was a long time ago. And if you are looking for a name, I don't have one. It was only the impression I had."

"What gave you that impression?"

"I remember wondering why someone would rifle through my stock of herbs," she said and looked over my shoulder to the door as though to make sure we were not overheard. She continued in a whisper. "And I remember wondering why someone would steal rue."

"Rue?" Thoughts of Hamlet and Ophelia rushed through my head. In the play, rue was the only flower Ophelia had given to herself. Had Alice drowned herself after all? "Rue for regret?" I said, trying to remember the flower's meaning.

Mrs. Harlan shook her head. "Rue has always been used by women for one purpose; to make themselves regular again." She gave me a meaningful look, then turned her attention back to the platter of sandwiches with the air of one who would say no more on the subject.

It took me a moment to comprehend her meaning, but once I did, the significance was clear. The summer Alice had died, a woman had stolen rue to end her pregnancy. My mind jumped to the happy summer Margaret Yardley had told me about. Which of the three young women had been pregnant?

Mrs. Harlan picked up her platter and paused by my side on her way out of the kitchen. "Ever since the Major came back, strange things have been going on in this village. And now, Eliot Yardley's conservatory was broken into." She looked at me as though she knew something more.

I jumped. "When?" I asked defensively. Had Mrs. Harlan observed me coming out of the Dowager's House? Though with a sinking feeling, I now realized I'd completely overlooked a search of the conservatory. Perhaps I had not been as thorough as I'd thought.

"I heard him say that it happened last night," she said and nodded her head towards the parlor. "And I hear the same thing happened at Lord Tatham's not long ago," she added. "The Major coming back here was a bad omen."

Relaxing, I nodded. "Yes, something strange is going on."

I followed Mrs. Harlan out of the kitchen, determined to speak to Eliot Yardley. I wondered if something had been taken from the conservatory and how it would fit in with all the other clues.

The barrister was easy to pick out from among the guests as I paused at the doorway. A small circle had gathered around him, and he towered at least a head above his listeners. He was recounting vociferously the events from the conservatory, perhaps for anyone who hadn't heard about the incident quite yet. His voice carried.

"Nothing was taken, you see!" He chortled. "They had left something."

The surrounding assembly tittered, as though they wanted to laugh at the punchline, but were conscious that they were also at a funeral.

I nodded to Dr. Perkins as I threaded my way among the guests, making for Eliot Yardley. The next moment, however, I glimpsed something distressing. My breath caught. I pushed my way further into the room with some urgency. My target came in and out of view as people shifted this way and that. My pulse quickened, and I could hear the blood rushing in my ears. I knew it was too much to hope that the fluffy white hair sprouting over the top of a wing chair would belong to Mr. Graves.

I rounded the chair, and my heart sank. There, sitting quite contentedly with an overflowing plate in his lap, was Uncle Albert.

"Ah, Caroline!," he chirped when he noticed me. "At last. Glad you were able to make it."

I bent towards Uncle and whispered, "What are you doing here?"

"I hardly think I could have missed Richard's funeral," he said. "He was my kin, after all."

I was about to ask him if he'd forgotten about our plan, but that likelihood was self-evident. Plus, I didn't want his attacker to know that...that what? None of the plan mattered any more. It was quite obvious to the attacker, if Uncle had been the target, that the poisonous pellet had missed and Uncle was not on his deathbed. At least, a glance about the room told me that Mr. Graves had kept to the house.

"How did you get here?" I asked Uncle. He never went anywhere without Wilford.

"The stable boy drove." He waved a hand in an indeterminate direction. "Jolly good driver, if a tad fast."

Eliot Yardley sidled up to me. "Bertie told me about the attack on Mr. Graves," he said under his breath. I didn't get the opportunity to send a scathing glance at Uncle before he added, "What the devil is going on?"

"I don't know," I said truthfully.

"Ah, that's where I'm ahead of you," Eliot

Yardley said, perking up a bit. "I think you probably haven't heard what occurred in my conservatory?"

I shook my head.

"Well, it was Julia who in fact discovered it." He glanced in his wife's direction, who was holding court with a group that could be nothing other than the church's flower ladies. "Julia had gone to the conservatory to retrieve the wreath we'd ordered for Richard, and she noticed that someone had been there. Moved things around. It's the damndest thing. Very much like the thing that happened at Bertie's greenhouse. But here is the essential point: instead of taking something, they'd left something." He paused as though for effect.

"What?"

"A chemistry set."

I frowned. "What?"

The barrister's countenance became serious, and he glanced at Uncle. "Do you know what a chemistry blowpipe kit is, Lady Caroline?"

The term was familiar to me. I searched my brain, trying to locate anything relevant from chemistry lessons.

Eliot Yardley didn't wait for me. "It's a kit of tools used to analyze substances. It comes in a wooden box and is usually given to young boys to subject rocks and minerals to a flame, to see what elements one can detect. We had one as boys, not sure where it got to, I suppose might be the same box...Anyhow, the material point is that the kit comes with a small metal blowpipe. One blows through it on the flame of a burner to intensify it, like a blowtorch."

I was listening most intently.

"It is that pipe that is missing from the kit," Eliot Yardley said.

I stared at him. "Are you saying...?"

He nodded. "It won't stand up in court, of course. Especially since the pipe is missing. But I bet that was how Mr. Graves was attacked yesterday."

We exchanged a look. He didn't have to say it. We both understood that this had also been the method employed to poison the Major.

Now we had the method. But where were the berries?

"Break-ins, thefts," Julia Yardley's voice floated over to me. "Take care of the small crimes, I say, and the big ones will take care of themselves."

I smirked. Had I not believed all these petty crimes were connected with the Major's murder, I might have thought them orchestrated by someone standing for the magistrate's post.

I cast a glance about the room. At least the place was too crowded for the killer to try another attack on Uncle.

CHAPTER 19

The stable boy, Thomas, drove us back to the Hall. He handled Uncle's Silver Ghost in a way I never knew possible. Even Wilford's words of warning delivered sternly at the driver's left elbow could not dampen the lad's enthusiasm, and the Rolls Royce hurtled around corners with surprising agility.

At first, Uncle was rather delighted with the joyride, but by the time we arrived at the Hall, his visage was positively green. By dinnertime, it transpired that Uncle's color-change was not entirely due to Thomas' dexterity with the steering wheel, and the doctor was called to the Hall once more.

"His pulse is weak," Dr. Perkins said after he'd finished his examination.

Uncle was lying in bed, much like Mr. Graves had been the previous day. But unlike his cousin, Uncle really was not feeling well. Sweat beaded on his brow, and his white hair hung in limp filaments around his face. His breathing was labored.

"I do not want to worry you, Lady Caroline," the doctor said, "but I believe Lord Tatham has been poisoned."

I just about managed to find a chair, and slumped into it as my legs gave way under me.

"Do you think he was shot with a poisonous pellet like Mr. Graves?" I asked feebly. Words that the doctor had uttered the previous day rushed back to me—even the smallest grain of the rosary pea poison would be fatal, and there was no antidote. "But how is it possible?" I added. The family had been together at the funeral and the reception. No one would have been brazen enough to take out a blowpipe to shoot at Uncle. Unless the culprit had not been among those attending the funeral. What if Mr. Graves, who I'd assumed had stayed in the house, had in fact followed Uncle and shot at him? The maids, however, had mentioned that he had not left his room all day, preferring to run them off their feet with silly requests instead.

"I don't think it's the rosary pea," the doctor said. "I couldn't find any cuts on His Lordship's skin." He glanced again at Uncle. "My best guess is that he was poisoned by something that was slipped in his food or drink at the reception. He takes his tea strong. Perhaps he would not have noticed anything amiss. I've administered some charcoal, but I'm afraid that is all I can do without knowing what the poison is."

"Is there any hope?" I asked.

The doctor hung his head. I was struck by how much he'd aged in the last few hours. Dark shadows had gathered about his eyes, and the furrows between his brows had deepened. "Once the symptoms set in, I'm afraid there's very little a doctor can do," he said. "I'm sorry."

We sat in silence for a little while, then he got up and picked up his Gladstone bag. "Do you want me to inform His Lordship's brothers?"

I shook my head vehemently. "I prefer to do it," I said, though I had no intention of doing so at the moment. One of them could be the killer. I didn't want them anywhere near Uncle this night.

The doctor paused at the door, turning back to me. "I wonder if we should have involved the police yesterday after all, as you'd suggested. Perhaps it's advisable to call the police now."

I nodded. I tried to stay coherent for the doctor. But I wasn't fully listening. Inside, I was barely holding myself together. The doctor left.

I glanced at Wilford, who'd been standing by the door, frozen in rigid incapacity, staring at the bed where the limp figure of Uncle lay. Uncle's faithful servant now looked at me expectantly, awaiting my instructions. For a moment, he appeared as though about to speak, but I shook my head to forestall any inquiries.

What point was there in calling the police? They'd only plod around the house, asking questions I was in no state to answer, disturbing

Uncle's final hours. There was plenty of time tomorrow to deal with all of this. A few hours would make no difference. By now, the killer would have disposed of the poison, the washing up at the Vicarage would have been done, and any evidence of poison would have disappeared down the drain.

Wilford went around the room and turned out the lights, then took a chair closer to Uncle's bed to join my vigil. As the room plunged into darkness, save for a single light by Uncle's bedside, I gave way to my darkest thoughts.

Could I have prevented this? How silly my plan to search the houses of Uncle's step-brothers seemed now. I'd found nothing. I should have stayed with Uncle, making sure that he was safe until I'd discovered who the killer was.

Ought I to have heeded the doctor's advice and kept out of it altogether? I cast about in my mind. Had Uncle's poisoning been brought about by anything I'd done? No, at least on that point I was blameless. The moment Uncle had found the Major's body in the library, his fate had been sealed. The killer suspected that something had transpired between Uncle and the Major that fateful night. And that made Uncle a threat to be eliminated.

I closed my eyes and leaned my head against the chair back. All I could do for Uncle now was to find the killer.

What pieces of evidence had I gathered so far?

To start with, there were the break-ins. The greenhouse—most likely for access to a poison. But presumably, that had failed. Then the house—for the silver bracelet.

I'd given the bracelet little thought, I conceded. Why had I not asked one of Uncle's brothers about it? But what role did the bracelet play in the murders? And where was that bracelet now? Was it with the missing locket?

I willed my mind back to the evidence I did have. A third break-in had occurred at the barrister's conservatory. But instead of taking something, the culprit had left a chemistry kit, crucially with its blowpipe missing. It seemed as though the killer had started planting evidence on others. I was certain the blowpipe was how the Major was poisoned. And yet, a problem remained. How had the killer obtained the rosary pea poison?

Then, there was the locket. The Major had given it to Alice. She had taken it off before her death. Coupled with the letter she'd been writing, this had led her mother to believe that Alice had taken her own life. The inquest had ruled the death an accident, so why had I initially thought that Alice had drowned herself? Had it been my aunts' doing, with their talk of tragic events? No. The impression had been created during dinner that first night. But who had created it? And why insist Alice had taken her life, if the official verdict was accidental death?

Based on the doctor's records, however, I suspected that Alice had been murdered. And the killer had left the note on the shore to make her death look like suicide.

According to Margaret Yardley, it was the locket that had prompted the Major to come back to the village and look into Alice's death. Alice's mother had given the locket to Margaret. Margaret had given it back to the Major. The necklace had made a full circle, but where was it now?

The conversations I'd had with the doctor, Alice's mother, and even Margaret Yardley, had left me with the strong impression of a love triangle. I suspected Dr. Perkins had been in love with the girl. But he'd been away from the village when Alice had died. And so had Julia. Had the Vicar or the barrister been in love with Alice as well? I had been reluctant to ask too many questions of the family, for fear of revealing that I believed one of them was responsible for the Major's death.

There was also the evidence from Alice's mother that someone had stolen rue from her herb stock. Was that evidence that one of the three women had been pregnant that summer? Or had it been a young woman entirely unconnected to this case? Whoever she had been, had she succeeded in making herself regular again? Based on the doctor's notes, it had not been Alice. According to Alice's mother, Margaret had been quite ill around the time of Alice's death. And according to Margaret, Julia had been away, leaving a tomboy and coming back beautiful.

But what if the Major's death had nothing to do with Alice? What if it were connected to the incident in India the barrister had mentioned? The Vicar had assured me that it was an accident and no one had died. But in private, he seemed to harbor some doubts. What if the Major had discovered something incriminating in India and had come to confront the Vicar and his wife with it?

I took some time to go over my pieces of evidence again. I was beginning to suspect that I had caught someone out in a lie. I was beginning to see the killer more clearly.

For a while, I watched Uncle come in and out of a state of delirium. Wilford dabbed his brow with a cold towel. Eventually, I must have fallen asleep.

I woke up disoriented, squinting against a bright light that hurt my eyes. It was morning. I was curled up in the easy chair. Someone had thrown a blanket over me. For a moment my mind was muddled, but then I glanced at Uncle's bed and jolted upright. The bed was empty. I flung the blanket aside and jumped out of my chair. Wilford was also gone.

What had happened to Uncle?

I rushed out of the room and down the corridor and descended the stairs at a run. Where was everybody? At the bottom of the stairs, I glanced at the grandfather clock and halted. It was barely past six o'clock in the morning—too early for the servants to be in this part of the house. I stood and listened. No one seemed to be about. I pushed through the green baize door to the servants' quarters.

From the kitchen, the smell of something baking wafted towards me. Plates and cutlery clattered, accompanied by the rhythmic tapping of a whisk against a bowl. I popped my head round the kitchen door. Cook and the maids were busy getting ready for breakfast. All appeared so everyday and normal. Had Wilford told them what had happened to Uncle Albert?

Noticing me, Cook started. "Oh, you gave me a fright, my lady. I didn't expect you up so early."

The maids got up and curtsied. I had interrupted their bread and tea.

"Breakfast won't be ready for another two hours," Cook continued, "but I can whip you up something quick. Some eggs, perhaps?"

I shook my head. "No, thank you." I frowned, perplexed by her casual manner at such a time. Surely the staff knew that Uncle had been poisoned.

Cook mirrored my countenance and frowned at the bowl she was whipping. "So many strange goings-on since Major Yardley came back. Alive one day, and then, poof!" She gave an extra-hard stir to her batter to underscore her point. "And now, Lord Tatham. It's as if he was never..." She shook her head again, and spoke to the bowl. "I just don't understand how it could happen so quickly."

Tears filled my eyes. I had to leave the kitchen before the staff could see me cry. "I was looking for Wilford," I said with a final semblance of normality.

"I believe you'll find him in the library, my lady," Hannah said.

My frown deepened. Why the library? The staff were acting as though nothing was out of the ordinary. But I couldn't bring myself to ask them about Uncle and what had happened. I made my way down the long, dark corridor towards the library. Confused thoughts swirled in my mind. Why had Uncle been moved out of his bed? Why had no one thought of rousing me? How could I have slept through it all?

I pushed open the heavy doors of the library. The room looked much as it had the first day I had visited. At a quick glance, I could not see Wilford. He was not in the gallery either. Then, my eyes fell on a figure in a dark cloak hunched over the desk in the window alcove. The hair glowed downy white in the morning light.

I stilled my breath as the head turned slowly. "Ah, Caroline! There you are. You sleep well, I trust?"

"Uncle Albert?" I asked.

He smiled at me beatifically, the morning light forming a halo around his head.

I walked further into the library. "But you were poisoned," I said. I approached cautiously and spoke softly, feeling as though he were a mirage, a specter that was going to dissolve into thin air. "You were so ill last night. The doctor thought you were dying."

"I told you Dr. Perkins was a fool." He waved a dismissive hand in the air, and the blanket around his shoulders that I had taken for a cloak slipped. "Never felt better. A slight metallic taste in the mouth, perhaps. And a bit of gastric distress, but one hears that's to be expected of Margaret." He sniggered and cast me a mischievous look. "Wilford telephoned the doctor first thing this morning. He's coming to give me the once-over and the all-clear shortly. Until then, I think Wilford has gone to have a bit of a lie-down, poor fellow." He chuckled again. "Cook got a bit of a shock as well when I went into the kitchen this morning. I was feeling rather peckish since I had missed dinner. If I didn't know better, I might think you had all written me off."

I let out a laugh, startling Uncle, and surprising myself as well. I was perhaps releasing all the nerves and worries that had coiled up inside me. There was no use asking Uncle how he'd done it, how he'd pulled through. I would have to wait for the doctor.

"What are you working on?" I said, sidling up to him. I had the urge to kiss the top of his head, as one might a child's, but I settled for a hand on his shoulder.

Uncle had a large magnifying glass propped up on the desk and was examining something resembling a small golden scarab under it.

"A locket," he said casually. "It's the locket Richard had in his hand when I found him in here the other morning."

"What?!" I cried in disbelief.

CHAPTER 20

I stared at Uncle. "So you've had the locket all along?!"

"I'd quite forgotten about it," he said. "It was only when I was rummaging through my pockets for a handkerchief this morning that I noticed it."

"May I see it?"

Uncle deposited it into my palm. It was an oval locket on a delicate gold chain. I closed my eyes, thinking back to all the items Uncle had taken out of his pockets in the greenhouse that first day. I sniggered. The locket had been among them. I'd mistaken it for a lorgnette chain with a fob, because why would Uncle have a golden locket? How silly of me. The brain's rather good at tricking us into seeing that which we expect.

"So much for my theory that if I found the locket, I'd find the killer," I said sardonically.

Uncle sent me a sly smile.

I'd put so much stock into this locket. I'd hoped that it would lead me to the killer. I wasn't ready to be disappointed further. I opened it slowly. Inside was the silhouette of a man.

"Do you know who this is?" I asked, although I could guess.

"That's Richard as a young man," Uncle said.

I nodded. Was that why Margaret Yardley had wanted the locket? Was that why she'd worn it for twenty years? Because it contained the Major's portrait? The love triangle, I reminded myself. Margaret had been in love with Richard. I wondered if the Vicar knew?

"But why did you take it off the Major?" It was a rather curious behavior. Uncle was not known to be a magpie.

He looked at me with shifty eyes. "I simply thought it was something that Richard had pocketed from the curio cabinet."

"You thought he was the one who had broken into the curio cabinet," I said.

"Well, it happened soon after he arrived in the village," Uncle said rather defensively and shrugged his weak shoulders. "But upon closer examination, it doesn't appear to be something that my father would have kept in a curio cabinet." He fell silent for a bit. "Although, Richard was his favorite son. If he could have, I think Father would have given the title to Richard. He admired his beauty and strength. But I was safely ensconced in Burma for a time, and then Hong Kong, and Ceylon." He gave a self-satisfied smile, safe in the knowledge that nothing short of a guillotine could unseat him from his primogeniture.

"You know, there was something else about it," he said after a moment. "Richard was holding the locket as though he wanted me to have it. He had it hanging from his outstretched hand, as though he knew he was dying and wanted whoever found him to have it."

"Like a clue," I said.

But a clue to what? The killer or the reason for his murder?

The Major must have known he'd been poisoned and dying. How much had the Major figured out about Alice's death and about his own murder? Why had he not told anyone?

Perhaps that was why he'd wanted to speak to Uncle. Uncle was the only one in the family the Major could trust. Uncle was the only one who'd been out of the country when Alice had died. Uncle was the only one who could not possibly have murdered her. Or him. The Major had left the locket for Uncle to find, hoping he would continue looking into Alice's death. And his.

I wondered again why Margaret Yardley had wanted this locket so desperately. Only someone who was truly in love, or dangerously obsessed, would wear a locket of their secret love for twenty years. Which one was Margaret? Was Margaret Yardley a killer? Had she killed Alice, then again in India, and now the Major?

I cupped the locket in my hand, watching

the chain pool like a drop of water in my palm. I probably should have guessed sooner that Margaret had been secretly in love with Richard; that this was the reason Margaret had wanted the locket for herself. I wondered if the Vicar knew about Richard's picture inside it?

I must admit, however, that I didn't feel the locket brought me any closer to solving the mystery of Alice's death, or the Major's. And yet, the locket seemed to have been very important to the Major. It had brought him to the village, and he had held it in his hand when he'd died. What had he wanted to communicate? What was I missing? What was I not understanding about the locket?

"You know, Caroline," Uncle was saying. He was looking down at something on the other side of him. "I don't know why you had the gardeners running around the estate yesterday collecting red berries."

He picked up a basket from the floor and placed it in his lap. Inside, clusters of juicy red berries, ripe and glistening, nestled among bright green leaves.

"Fred brought the cuttings to me just a few minutes ago. You seemed to have impressed upon him the importance of the task, and once he heard I was out and about, probably from Cook, he rushed to deliver the basket." Uncle's tone suggested that I had wasted the gardeners' time.

"There must be a rosary pea growing on the

estate somewhere," I said rather defensively.

Uncle shook his head. "I told you it's not possible. What you have here is *Sorbus aucuparia*, V*iburnum opulus*, *Ribes rubrum*, *Crataegus monogyna*," he listed off the species with ease as he dug through the basket. Then he placed it back on the ground. "And at any rate, why are you looking for red berries?"

I narrowed a suspicious glance at him. "What do you mean? The books on Indian flora say that the rosary pea has bright red berries." Though in truth, I hadn't actually read any of the books. I'd only been going by the description various people had given me. Who? I wondered suddenly. Eliot Yardley, certainly. But who else? Had the killer misled me about the berries?

"If you'd read the descriptions closely," Uncle was saying, "you'd know that the rosary pea can also have white berries."

"What?!" I said, surprised. But somewhere deep in my mind, a realization stirred.

"Come, let me show you," Uncle said.

I stared at Uncle as he raised himself with difficulty and shuffled towards the library door. He was not leading me towards the gardens, but back into the depths of the house. I followed him with trepidation. Where was he taking me? Was he about to reveal that, like the locket, the source of the rosary pea poison had been in one of his pockets all along?

Down the dark hallway we went, my mind suddenly blank. Uncle's unexpected expedition to the source of the white rosary pea had caused the idea I'd had to vanish. We entered the drawing room. I glanced around uneasily. Where could the rosary pea be hiding here?

Uncle stopped in front of one of the botanical drawings scattered among the browning oil portraits.

"Here it is, Caroline," he said, gazing up at a framed drawing of a plant. "*Abrus precatorius*, the rosary pea, with white seeds."

Indeed, the drawing showed an ink and watercolor rendition of the plant Uncle was growing for the flower show. It had the same delicate pink flowers and fine green leaves. The illustration had one advantage over Uncle's plant; it showed the seed pods. Red seeds were bursting out of dried brown casings. The characteristic black spot at the top of the seed indeed made them look like ladybirds. And next to the red seeds, the artist had illustrated white ones. About twice the size of the red ones, the white seeds looked like pearls, if one ignored the large black spot at the top.

I nodded as the clues began to fall into place. The idea from earlier had returned.

"Remind me, Uncle," I said, glancing about the room, "the day you had the Major and the rest of the family over for tea, were you gathered in this room?"

"Yes," he said.

"And do you remember who was sitting facing the drawing?"

He turned around to look at the chairs arranged around the room. "I can't recall with any certainty."

I had to find a way to help him remember. "Where were you sitting?"

"Here," he said, indicating a chair with its back to the drawing.

"And the chair was in this position that day?"

He nodded. "It always is."

I moved about the room, glancing at the illustration. "The drawing is visible to anyone not sitting with their back to it. So when you were telling your relations about growing the rosary pea, they could all see the representation of the plant above your head. And what's more, one of them recognized the white seeds." I shook my head in disbelief. "How could I have been so silly?" I said. "I saw those seeds yesterday and didn't recognize them."

Searching through the Vicar's and the barrister's belongings, I had been looking for a bracelet fit for an Indian princess. Not one made out of seeds. I mused once again about how our brains played tricks on us. To the maid, Lily, the bracelet, with its intricate silver clasp, displayed among treasures from around the Empire, had looked exotic and sumptuous. To me, when I had seen it yesterday, with its string broken and beads missing, it had looked like a discarded trinket.

Uncle was gazing at me with curiosity.

"Remember the bracelet that was taken from the curio case?" I said to Uncle. "It was made of white rosary pea seeds."

Perhaps I should have guessed the purpose of the bracelet earlier. Especially when the Vicar told me that natives used the seeds for jewelry.

"The killer, who was among the guests at tea that day," I continued, "had seen the bracelet many times before in the curio cabinet."

I did not elaborate that it had been Uncle telling everyone about the poisonous plant that had put the idea to use the bracelet in the killer's head.

"So it's one of the family?" Uncle asked.

I nodded. "At least we can eliminate the doctor," I said, "as he wasn't at tea that day." And Alice's mother, I added in my mind.

"Was he ever a suspect?" Uncle asked, surprised.

I shrugged in reply.

He frowned at me again. "Do you know who it is?"

I nodded. "I think I do. But proving it will not be easy. I need to go to the Vicarage."

And though I wanted to depart for the Vicarage immediately, I needed to wait for a more suitable hour. I ate breakfast, lost in thought, trying to arrange my ideas, with Uncle staring at me. Though I was sure he was curious to know more, he didn't pester me with questions.

All the evidence I'd collected was coming together. The bracelet, the blowpipe, and the locket. Yes, I was certain I'd figured out the significance of the locket now. I could not be sure if that was what the Major had had in mind when he'd held out the locket in his hand for Uncle to find, but it didn't matter. My interpretation of the importance of the locket helped me pick out the killer from among all the possible suspects, and from among all the various reasons for killing the Major.

I nodded, satisfied, and allowed myself a smirk. The killer had not understood the significance of the locket.

I drove to the Vicarage. It was safer than walking through the park, even though by now the killed had disposed of the murder implements. I doubted I'd be shot at with a poisonous pellet. But even so, one had to take precautions until the killer was caught.

At the Vicarage I was met by the Vicar at the door. "Ah! Lady Caroline," he said somewhat flustered. "I was just on my way to see Albert. I've only just heard. Why did no one inform us yesterday?"

I smiled noncommittally.

"At any rate," the Vicar continued, "I'm glad he's recovered. They say he was poisoned. I hope it wasn't anything he ate at the reception after the funeral."

"Actually, I'm here on a related matter," I said. "Is your wife in? I wanted to speak with her."

"Margaret?" the Vicar said, a sudden weariness washing over his face. "Why do you want to speak with Margaret? She's gone to her sister's for a few days," he said evasively. "I thought it best. She didn't take the news about Albert well at all. She's had an aversion to poisons ever since India..." he trailed off.

I nodded my understanding. I was sympathetic to Margaret's plight, but needed to be firm on this point. "I believe I know who poisoned the Major."

The Vicar's face darkened. He invited me in.

He listened patiently without interrupting as I explained my theory to him. He then reached into his pocket and took out a bracelet fashioned out of white seeds. It hung limply, almost pathetically, from his fingers. On one side of the broken circle was the string where a few seeds had been removed. On the other, was the silver clasp. It was difficult to believe that it was such a dangerous thing.

I nodded. This was the bracelet I'd seen in Margaret's jewelry case yesterday.

"I was looking for her locket this morning, while she was out in the garden," the Vicar said. "I noticed she'd stopped wearing it when Richard came back. I'd never looked inside…so I wondered…but instead, I found the bracelet. I recognized it and the seeds right away. I'd seen these seeds in India, of course. I sent Margaret away. She's with her sister until I can make arrangements for us to go away on a mission. It's better this way."

I looked at the bracelet in his hand again. "If justice is to be served, I think you need to call your wife back."

CHAPTER 21

The following day at teatime, Uncle Albert, Mr. Graves, and I gathered in the Vicarage together with the Major's brothers and their wives. The previous day, after speaking with the Vicar, who'd agreed to call his wife back, I'd gone to visit Eliot Yardley and his wife. I'd intimated to them that I knew who'd poisoned the Major. As this was a family matter, I'd said, all could be resolved without calling the police. Eliot Yardley had bristled somewhat at the notion of excluding the law, but as any well-bred Englishman, he had an aversion to publicity. And though he and his wife had tried to dissuade me, calling my actions foolish, even dangerous, curiosity had prevailed, and they had agreed to attend.

Under my recommendation, the Vicar's cook and maid were given the afternoon off. To the Vicar, I had made the suggestion under the guise of prudence. It was better, I'd said, for the staff not to overhear the family's affairs. In truth, however, I had set a plan in motion, and for it to work, only the family had to be present. The cook had prepared cakes and laid out the tea things, so all Margaret Yardley had to do was serve them.

Well before the appointed hour, I hid in the kitchen pantry, leaving the door ajar by the merest crack. As the guests began to assemble in the drawing room, I waited in the pantry, keeping an eye on the tea service. I was certain the killer would strike again.

I suspected the killer would be bringing an extract of a plant with them to the party, but I had prepared a botanical trick of my own.

"I am much obliged to you all for coming," I said, entering the drawing room not a minute after everyone had arrived and taking my seat beside Uncle.

In the hours leading up to the tea party, I had struggled with how I would go about revealing the killer, not because I had any doubts about the killer's identity, but because revealing their identity would inevitably lead to questions about motive. And revealing the truth about the motive was bound to hurt many innocent people.

Thus, I had decided to begin by laying out the method of the murder, hoping the killer would reveal themselves before I had to explain why they'd poisoned the Major.

"As you already know," I continued, "I believe I

have pieced together the identity and the motive of Major Yardley's killer. I'd like to begin, however, by explaining *how* the Major was murdered."

The Vicarage's drawing room was small, and we'd arranged ourselves around a low occasional table; except for Mr. Graves, who once again had elected to sit outside the family circle, and had positioned himself in a hardback chair against the wall. He'd agreed to participate rather reluctantly, but the chance to witness others' misfortunes was a powerful motivator.

I glanced at the rest of my suspects. Margaret Yardley, her face pallid, sat rigidly on the edge of a chair at one end of the table. She stared blankly through me. Across the table from her sat her husband, the Vicar. He was gazing at me darkly, his displeasure with my antics evident. On the sofa sat Eliot and Julia Yardley. Her look was defiant—head held high, looking down at me. It was clear she thought the whole thing silly and beneath her. Her husband wore a look reminiscent of an eager tennis partner, as though he relished the opportunity to object and argue against my case. Completing the intimate circle were Uncle and I, sitting in squashy armchairs across from the sofa.

Whatever Uncle had ingested during the funeral reception seemed to have acted like a revitalizing tonic. He had emerged from his brush with death with the alacrity of a newborn phoenix —his hair luscious, his eyes bright. He looked around with lively curiosity, mirroring Eliot Yardley's enthusiasm. If the killer was surprised to see Uncle in rude health, they didn't show it.

So far, no one had noticed that tea had not been served. No one perhaps except the killer, who glanced at the door once or twice. I pretended not to see.

"Almost from the moment of my arrival on Uncle's estate," I continued, "on the day Major Yardley's body was discovered in the library, I found myself drawn to the string of strange incidents which coincided with the Major's arrival in the village, and, perhaps more tellingly, preceded his death. At first, I could not understand how the seemingly unconnected break-ins at the greenhouse and at the Hall could have any bearing on the Major's death.

"Uncle assured me that nothing had been taken from the greenhouse. But then I learned that up until a fortnight before the break-in, a variety of poisonous distillates were stored at the greenhouse; a fact well known in the village. I wondered if it was those poisons the culprit had been after when they broke into the greenhouse. But what the killer had not known was that Dr. Perkins, fearing Uncle Albert could poison himself, had taken the distillates away. Rather discreet, the doctor had told no one about it. So the culprit had gone away empty-handed. But what this first break-in tells us, in hindsight, coinciding as it did with the Major's return, is that the killer had decided to murder the Major almost from the very moment the Major returned to the village."

I refrained from saying that this coincidence at first had led me to suspect the Major himself of the break-ins.

"Now we come to the second break-in. It happened the following night. This time, the curio cabinet in the Great Hall was burgled. For a while, I could not understand what connected the two events. And indeed, I didn't make the connection until yesterday. Why would a killer in search of poisons break into a curio cabinet? It was unfathomable. But the more important question is, what had taken place between these two events? And the answer is that Uncle had hosted his family for tea."

Uncle now stirred. "I say!" he protested.

I suppressed a sigh. Uncle had proven himself to be rather unreliable when it came to following directions. I hoped he'd remember enough of what I'd told him to keep himself safe. After all, I was doing all of this for his sake. Until the killer was caught, Uncle's life was in danger.

"To understand why a would-be killer, looking for poisons in a greenhouse, would then go on to break into a curio cabinet in the house, we have to go back to the afternoon of tea at the Hall. Unaware of the murderous intent of one of his guests, Uncle told everyone about the rosary pea plant he was growing and the poisonous seeds it produced. And there, hanging on the wall right behind him, was an illustration of the rosary pea, for all attending to see. The seeds of the rosary pea are rather singular, with a large black dot at the tip, which is especially noticeable on the white ones. And the killer recalled where they had seen a bracelet made of just such beads—the curio cabinet. So they stole it. That was rather clever. Even if someone realized that a bracelet had been stolen, as one of the maids did, no one would think that the bracelet itself was the source of the poison.

"The rest was rather easy for the killer. The instructions for preparing the poison are contained in a surprising number of books on Indian plants. The seeds are broken open, the poisonous pulp shaped into a sharp-tipped pellet, and left to dry for a day. Here the killer deviated from the books. Instead of delivering the poison through a sharp blow, they turned to a childhood skill, and shot the pellet into the Major's neck using a blowpipe taken from an old chemistry kit. A small cut on the Major's neck indicated where the arrowhead had pierced his skin. But the doctor dismissed the cut as irrelevant, as it had almost healed."

"But surely the Major would have seen his assailant," Eliot Yardley objected.

"Not necessarily," I countered, "as the attack

on Mr. Graves illustrates. If the assailant attacked from the edge of the woods, they could get very close to their victim without being observed. Like Mr. Graves, the Major probably assumed that he'd been stung by a bee. Even if he'd swiped at his neck, any piece of poison left under his skin would have been enough to kill him in a few days. As all the literature on the subject tells us, the poison is not only powerful, but also undetectable. A perfect weapon.

"What the killer had not counted on, however, was that Uncle's little speech had put others in mind of the poison. The Major, for one, who I believe became aware that he'd been poisoned. And Eliot Yardley, who was first to suggest that the Major had been willfully murdered. That must have been a blow to the killer. The poison was so clever, so clean. And to have Eliot Yardley spoil it so."

Eliot Yardley gave me a dubious smile. Perhaps he'd never considered that the killer might be rather unhappy with him over that little stunt.

"I wondered if I could narrow down the killer based on their knowledge of the rosary pea," I continued, "but it transpired that everyone knew about it. The Vicar and his wife had lived in the Bengal, ministered among the very people who used the poison so prevalently in their trade. The poison had so impressed the Vicar that he'd even written to his brother, Eliot, about it. Eliot Yardley, in turn, remembered those letters to this day, as he told us at dinner. Perhaps he even read them out to his wife," I said and smiled at Julia Yardley. She gave me a small nod. "With all the books available on Indian plants, each one of them practically a manual on how to prepare and administer the poison, no one could be eliminated simply on the grounds of lacking knowledge of the rosary pea."

I paused and glanced around. Was my killer riled enough? Not yet.

"Just as Eliot Yardley's pronouncement after dinner had been a devastating blow to the killer, so had the failure of the attack on Mr. Graves."

A few turned to look at the man.

"Yes, why was Mr. Graves attacked?" the Vicar asked.

"Because the killer mistook him for Uncle Albert," I said. "There is a striking resemblance between the two men. And the reason the killer wanted Uncle Albert dead, brings us to the very first in this series of unforeseen complications for the killer. The killer had expected the Major to die in his bed, and for the doctor to rule it a natural death. As indeed Dr. Perkins did. But the Major died in Uncle's library instead. And from that moment, the killer could never be certain whether something had not passed between the two men. As indeed it had.

"Perhaps the Major remembered Uncle's plant talk. Perhaps he recognized the symptoms from his time in India. Whatever the reason, the Major sent a message to Uncle, inquiring about the rosary pea. And though the killer was most likely unaware of this note, I believe the killer overheard Uncle confiding in me after dinner, on the night of my arrival. You see, Uncle was rather pleased that he'd kept the reason for the Major's presence in the library secret from his family."

I wondered for a moment if things might have turned out differently had Uncle not tried to be so secretive; had he been honest with his family that the Major had died before they could speak. But perhaps the killer would never have believed that the Major had made the trek to the library in his final hours without divulging to Uncle, perhaps in a note, any doubts and suspicions he might have had about his poisoner. Or Alice's killer.

"Albert, why would you do such a thing?" Eliot Yardley asked Uncle somewhat petulantly.

"Because as you said yourself, someone had poisoned Richard," Uncle countered. "I wasn't about to tell the murderer that Richard had been on to him."

I nodded, though Uncle was stretching the truth a bit. "Overhearing us, however," I continued, "had been enough to make the killer suspicious that Uncle knew more than he was letting on. Uncle had to be eliminated immediately. The killer waited by the greenhouse the next morning, but shot the wrong person.

What a disaster for our villain! Not only had the assailant attacked the wrong person, but Mr. Graves had survived. Growing desperate, the killer tried again at the funeral. With so many people about, and plates and drinks passed around, it would be easy to slip something poisonous in Uncle's fare, and hard to prove who'd actually done it. But Uncle Albert miraculously survived."

I turned and smiled at Uncle, and he beamed back at me. But I could feel that the energy in the room had shifted, and my listeners were growing restless. I needed to get on with it.

"The killer was clever enough to know that with the failed attempt on Mr. Graves, they had to get rid of the rosary pea evidence, disposing of the bracelet that was the source of the seeds, and the chemistry kit that was the source of the blowpipe. But here, the killer made yet another mistake. They planted the bracelet in Margaret Yardley's jewelry box."

I stilled my breath, waiting for someone to ask me how I knew the bracelet had been planted. Luckily, no one did. I didn't want to reveal that on the day I'd left my gloves behind at the Vicarage, and had returned to retrieve them, I'd used the opportunity of the Vicar and his wife having lunch to sneak up to their bedroom. I'd searched Margaret's jewelry box, hoping to find the missing locket. At that time, the bracelet had not been in the box. I'd searched her jewelry box again during the reception the following day, and the bracelet was now in the box, but I'd paid it no attention. Later, however, after learning that the beads of the bracelet were in fact poisonous seeds, I'd come to realize that the bracelet must have been planted in the box by the killer. The killer had perhaps used the diversion of the reception, just as I had, as a cover to sneak upstairs.

"But if all the evidence you are citing was planted by the killer on the innocent," the Vicar said, his voice rising in anger, "it can't possibly give you any clues as to the identity of the killer."

"What if these were clever subterfuges?" I countered. "After all, who would suspect that Eliot Yardley was the killer, when he was the one who suggested the Major was poisoned? Who would suspect Julia Yardley of using a blowpipe, when she was the one who discovered the chemistry kit in her conservatory? If Margaret Yardley was the killer, would she leave the incriminating bracelet in her jewelry box? And was the Vicar likely to poison Uncle Albert at a reception held at the Vicarage?" I paused for dramatic effect. "One of these things, however, was a bluff—the killer incriminated themselves in order to place themselves beyond suspicion."

CHAPTER 22

"Lady Caroline," Eliot Yardley said, his tone somewhat sardonic. "Surely you don't think one of the family killed Richard. What about Mrs. Harlan? Everyone knows she dabbles in poisons and holds him responsible for Alice's death. She had plenty of opportunity to drug him while he was staying at the Inn."

"Yes," I said. "But if we agree that the Major was poisoned with the rosary pea, and the poison came from the bracelet in the curio cabinet, only a member of the family, someone who had intimate knowledge of the contents of the curio cabinet—someone who'd grown up at the Hall, perhaps?—could have known where to get rosary pea seeds."

"So who is the killer?" the Vicar said bleakly.

I glanced at the clock on the mantelpiece.

"Lady Caroline, if you know who it is, what are you waiting for?" Eliot Yardley asked.

"The tea," I said quite innocently. "Perhaps now is a good time to serve the tea," I said, turning to the Vicar's wife.

Margaret Yardley gave me a startled look, but got up and left the room. A strained silence hung over us until she came back in with the tea things. The stillness was made even more evident by the sharp rattling of the cups and spoons on the overlarge tray as the Vicar's wife endeavored to set it down on the table. As her hands were shaking quite badly, I offered to pour the tea. Her nervousness seemed rather contagious, and people gazed around uncomfortably as the teacups were passed. I made certain to hand a cup of tea to Mr. Graves. His smirk upon receiving it was seen only by me.

We sipped in silence. I cast a furtive glance around. Was everyone drinking? Was anyone worried that there might be poison in the tea? But even the killer was taking quite a big gulp from their teacup. The killer's commitment to the theatrics was commendable. I allowed myself a sly smile and took another sip. But at that moment, a most unexpected tickle rose up in my throat.

Conceit comes before the fall, I mused darkly.

I coughed and set my teacup down. Around me, others began to cough as well. My breathing became short, and I found it difficult to take another breath. I clutched at my throat. I could not take another breath. I could not call out for help. I stared around in panic and was met with panicked looks in return. I heard a teacup fall to the ground and a spoon tinkle in a saucer. I willed myself to turn my head, but my head felt heavy. I was growing paralyzed and scared. My body was leaden, and my limbs refused to move. The effort to fight against the poison, which was now surely coursing through my body, was exhausting me, and I leaned back in my chair, ready to let the poison take over.

I closed my eyes, and all was black. Soon, all the noise in the room had ceased.

It was difficult to say how much time had passed, but suddenly I heard the faintest stirring. I eased one eyelid barely open, enough to see from behind my eyelashes.

Another hitch in the killer's plan. I suppressed a smirk. The killer's performance was about to begin.

"What's happened?" Eliot Yardley said. "Julia, are you quite alright? Julia?" He was shaking her arm.

She stirred at last as though awakening from a deep sleep. "There must have been something in the tea," she said, her voice drowsy.

I turned my eye behind the curtain of eyelashes towards her. Through the slit, I could see her looking about the room. She still seemed stunned and did not dare rise from her seat. I swiveled my eye around as far as it would go. The Vicar, his wife, Uncle, and his cousin all lay slumped in their chairs.

Julia finally got the courage to get up from her

seat. The clinking of porcelain told me that she was gathering some of the tea things. She had slipped her gloves back on.

"What are you doing?" Eliot Yardley asked.

"Getting rid of the tea," his wife said.

"Why?"

"Because it was poisoned."

"You mean everyone else is dead?"

"Yes."

"What have you done?" the barrister asked cautiously.

"What I had to," Julia Yardley hissed back at him.

I could just about see Eliot Yardley. His surprise had pinned him to his seat. Rotating his head slowly, he was taking a rather stunned look about the room, pausing on each body. As realization began dawning on him, his eyes became more alert.

"But how are you going to explain that we are the only people who survived?" he finally said. "Won't it look suspicious?"

Julia Yardley paused fiddling with the crockery for a moment, as though thinking. "Yes, that is a complication." Then she added, "But everyone knows I don't take sugar in my tea. And I'm about to add the poison to the sugar cubes. Then I'll wash out the pot, and our two teacups, and make new tea. When the police come, the poison will be only in the teacups of the others and in the sugar. No one will ever know that it was the tea that was poisoned. You and I did not take sugar, and are thus the only ones to miraculously survive."

Eliot Yardley watched his wife dumbly, with a look of utter incomprehension.

Julia Yardley went on, unperturbed. "Margaret, poor her. With her nerves. And with that accident in India. Everyone will think she did it. That she poisoned us. By mistake, of course. Such a tragedy." She resumed bustling with the tea things.

"When did you add the poison?" her husband asked.

"So silly to leave the pot in the kitchen unattended," she said in a singsong voice, as though delighting in the opportunity fortune had presented her with. "With the maid out for the day, I stopped by the kitchen and added it to the teapot. Monkshood is odorless and tasteless. No one would have noticed."

Eliot Yardley frowned at his wife. "Monkshood? Where did you even get such a thing?" He managed to sound more affronted by the inference that his wife had an unexpectedly thorough understanding of poisons, rather than by the fact that she'd killed the rest of the family to cover up the murder of the Major.

"From Mrs. Harlan. But I've learned a thing or two. This time, I made sure she didn't notice anything gone from her stock. I replaced her monkshood tincture with cooking oil. I used it on Arthur first, at the reception, but he survived somehow. Not this time." She paused and glanced around. "Though I must admit, it worked faster than I anticipated. I only pretended to take a big gulp of tea. No liquid touched my lips. Amateur dramatics is really paying off." She then looked at her husband and frowned. "But why did the poison have no effect on you?"

"I'm not certain," he said. And then, I saw the moment he finally comprehended the full extent of what he was witnessing. Confusion and denial rippled across his face in quick succession. "Julia," he began tentatively. "If the tea was poisoned...and you didn't warn me...you were going to poison me as well!" His voice had grown quite alarmed at the realization. "You were going to let me die!" he yelled.

"Darling, don't be so dramatic. I would have thought of some way to save you."

He didn't look convinced.

"I couldn't tell you," Julia said quite calmly. "It was the only way to make it look convincing. It would have looked quite suspicious if we'd both survived." She paused and looked around. I wondered if she truly realized the magnitude of what she'd done. "You, with your talk about the rosary pea. I warned you not to say anything about it. I blame those silly law books of yours. Always looking for the worst in people. If you hadn't blabbed, all would still be normal. Well, Bertie would have had to go. But now I'm presented with a challenge. It does look suspicious."

She sat back down on the sofa next to her husband, her eyes narrowed, her brow furrowed. He watched her with ever-increasing apprehension.

"It's actually better this way," she finally said. "Yes. No one knows we are here. We'll wash our two cups and then we'll leave. The maids are not here. No one would ever know we were here. And just think! You'll be Lord Tatham now. It's better than I could have ever hoped. I'm glad you are alive!" She patted his hand with her gloved one. He stared down at their joined hands mutely, as though his appendage was not attached to his body.

I'd let the whole thing go on for long enough. I cleared my throat and sat up. "That is enough now. It's over," I said.

"You!" Julia turned to me, her eyes wide. "How are you alive?"

But at that moment, the rest of the family began coming out of their stupors.

"Finally," Uncle said, straightening up as far as his back would allow. "I think my leg has gone to sleep."

Others mumbled appreciation for not having to pretend they were dead any longer.

"I thought I was going to sneeze," Margaret

Yardley said with a small giggle.

Julia Yardley looked around her with a rather crazed look, her eyes wide, her face growing ashen.

"I was in the kitchen, hiding. I observed you adding the poison to the pot," I said. "I'd instructed Margaret to serve an entirely different teapot. One porcelain teapot with flowers is much like another. I brought one over from the Hall. No one drank the poisoned tea. The poisoned teapot is still in the kitchen."

A change came over Julia Yardley, fear was swiftly replaced by a smug smile. She leveled a sly glance at me. "You can't prove it was me," she said.

"But we all heard you, Julia," Margaret said quietly. "And Lady Caroline saw you."

Julia Yardley turned to her sister-in-law slowly, as though a predator zeroing in on its prey. Her smile widened, and she bared her teeth. "What did she see, Margaret? As she said, one teapot is much like another. She can't prove anything. And as you all drank perfectly normal tea, and are all quite alive, there is nothing to charge me with."

"But your prints are on the teapot with the poison," I said. "And only your prints."

Julia Yardley gave me a pitying look. "If you were observing me, Lady Caroline, from your hiding place," she said with disdain, "you would have noticed that I wore gloves." She raised her hands and tinkled her gloved fingers.

"Ah yes, you wore gloves in the kitchen," I said,

sounding defeated. "But what you didn't know was that I'd taken care to coat the outside of the teapot all over with the pollen of *Neotinea lactea*. It's a rather rare orchid, found only on the sunny sea cliffs of the French Riviera. And in Uncle Albert's greenhouse. And its pollen is rather sticky. It would be all over your gloves." I looked at the place where her gloves had lain in her lap during tea. A faint dusting of pale yellow pollen marred the spot. "And all over your clothes. And the poison bottle. Pollen is as good as a fingerprint. Each species has a unique pollen grain shape that would be clearly visible under a police microscope."

"Why did you do such a wicked thing, Julia?!" Eliot Yardley cried. He gazed at his wife with a puzzled detachment, as though searching in her face for any trace of the person he'd known.

She raised her head defiantly at him and remained silent.

"It was because the Major—" I began. But at that moment Julia swerved her head to me. There was pleading in her eyes, as though she were begging me not to reveal the truth.

I glanced around at those gathered, and at Uncle by my side. All were staring at me, waiting for the truth. But if the truth came out, the rumors, the Press, it would devastate them.

"It was for the Major's money." I said.

Julia let out a gentle sigh and closed her eyes.

Then she opened them again and looked at

me. I lifted a challenging eyebrow. I was sure she understood that if she fought the charges that were about to be made against her, I would not hesitate to reveal the real reason why she killed the Major.

The Vicar went to telephone the police. Julia sat quite primly, head high, avoiding eye contact, while we waited for them to arrive.

It was the local constable who led Julia Yardley away a few minutes later. Eliot Yardley went with her, as her counsel.

The constable telephoned for reinforcements to help collect statements and evidence. We remained in the drawing room of the Vicarage, not touching anything, as instructed, to await the arrival of the inspector.

The comprehension that the ordeal was over spread around the room like a wave. People began chattering most happily.

"I was quite skeptical of your plan," said Mr. Graves. He'd moved his chair to sit near us. "I didn't think it would work." I smiled at him. Despite his doubts, he'd nevertheless made a pretty good corpse.

"Oh, I was so scared that I would pick up the wrong teapot," Margaret Yardley said. She giggled nervously.

"You did brilliantly," I said.

"How did you convince Julia?" the Vicar asked. "I mean, how did you know she'd add poison to the tea?" He was still frowning at me. He'd been unhappy with my plan from the beginning. Not only because it was dangerous and unlikely to succeed but also because it had taken its inspiration from Margaret's incident in India with the two kettles. He'd worried about how his wife would react to my plan, especially since she needed to play such a crucial role in it. Margaret Yardley had turned out to be a most willing participant, if a tad nervous. I believe she'd hoped to exorcise old ghosts.

I had explained my plan to everyone yesterday, except to Eliot Yardley and his wife. I'd instructed the partakers to follow my lead. Once I'd begun coughing, everyone else was supposed to act as though they'd been poisoned as well. I'd known that Julia was the killer, but I could not prove it. Or rather, I had no time to collect all the proof I needed. She'd tried to kill Uncle Albert twice. I had to make her incriminate herself before she had a chance to succeed.

"The power of suggestion," I said, answering the Vicar's question. "I went to a Swiss finishing school with a rather singular headmistress. She taught us all about the emerging field of psychoanalysis, with a particular focus on the theories of Carl Jung, a fellow Swiss, relating to word association and unconscious influences. While visiting Julia Yardley yesterday, I made sure to talk about the incident in India with the switched kettles. I also mentioned that I thought Margaret was the killer, since the poisonous bracelet was discovered in her jewelry box. Thus, I seeded the idea in her mind of poisoning the tea and blaming it on a terrible mistake by Margaret. Neither Margaret nor anyone else would be alive to say differently."

"But why kill all of us?"

"I believe she panicked. She had thought her plan to kill the Major using the rosary pea was perfect. She had not considered that anything could go wrong. But once it did, she hurried to distance herself from the crime. By getting rid of the evidence, however, she actually presented us with all the clues we needed to solve the murder. Her actions suggested she was worried people would soon begin putting the clues together. She couldn't even trust her husband, since he'd been the first to point out that Richard had been poisoned, and had guessed from the first what poison had been used."

"And all for Richard's money," the Vicar said, shaking his head in disbelief.

I remained silent on that point.

"Which one was the bluff?" Mr. Graves asked. "You said one of the clues was a bluff."

"It was the chemistry kit with the missing blowpipe," I said. "It had belonged to the Yardley brothers as children. Julia Yardley pretended that the killer had left it in the conservatory as a way to incriminate her and her husband."

The inspector then arrived, and the rest of the day went by in a blur as we gave statements.

So shocked was Uncle's family by what had transpired that no one had bothered to ask why the Major had returned to the village in the first place.

CHAPTER 23

"If you permit my saying so, my lady, your way of catching a killer was rather foolhardy," Wilford said. "The situation could have proved disastrous."

"We were never in any real danger," I said. "And after Uncle was attacked, I had to act. Julia Yardley would have tried again. I had to stop her."

Wilford and I were in the garden the day following Julia Yardley's arrest, watching Uncle potter about as we discussed the murder.

"His Lordship survived one poisoning," Wilford said loyally.

"He was unlikely to survive another," I objected.

Though Dr. Perkins was still baffled by Uncle's complete recovery, he had proposed a theory. Brewing distillates for years in his greenhouse, Uncle had been inadvertently exposing himself to, and sometimes even ingesting, small amounts of poison. Thus, he'd built up a resistance to all sorts of poisons. A dose that would have been fatal to others had merely made him unwell for a night.

"How did you know the killer was Julia

Yardley?" Wilford asked.

"The realization came on slowly. I'd built a case, or at least, I had identified a motive for every person I suspected. The crucial moment was when I learned that the poison had come from the stolen bracelet. That was when I knew the killer had to be a woman. As you and Uncle proved, only a woman would notice a bracelet among all other curios in the cabinet."

"And Julia Yardley's motive wasn't money, was it?" Wilford said.

"No. I only suggested that motive because I wanted to avoid a drawn-out scandal in the newspapers. The public is used to titled families fighting over money and killing each other over an inheritance. They will forget about this occurrence in a week, when the next greedy heir does something nefarious."

Wilford allowed himself a small smile.

"The real reason was love," I continued. "Or perhaps jealousy. Whatever it was, at the root of the murder was an affair of the heart. And it all began with Alice.

"I learned from Margaret Yardley that the family's encounter with Major Yardley in London had been quite unexpected. It seemed as though the Major had come to collect his money without any intention of visiting his relatives. He had not told any of them he was coming to England. But something about that chance meeting prompted the Major to make a trip to the village. It was because he saw Margaret Yardley wearing a locket he'd given as a parting gift, as a promise to return, to his beloved Alice.

"I can only guess what went through the Major's mind when he saw the locket, but it would be reasonable to assume that he was surprised. Perhaps even a little puzzled. He had learned about the death of Alice in a letter from the Vicar. He never had cause to question the veracity of the events described in the letter, namely, that Alice had drowned accidentally, until that moment. But seeing Margaret with the locket he'd gifted to Alice must have perplexed him. Certainly, it brought him to the village. Here, he met with Margaret, demanded back the locket from her, and set about inquiring into Alice's death.

"From Dr. Perkins, I learned that even though Alice's death had been ruled an accident, there had been some bruising on her head. It was just possible, I reasoned, that someone had killed her. But Alice's mother believed her daughter had taken her own life. Why? Because Alice had left behind a note and the locket Richard had given her. It was this locket that bothered me. It seemed like the key to the mystery. I now realize that the locket troubled me because it pointed to an inconsistency in Julia Yardley's story I had not noticed at first.

"On the night of my arrival, after dinner, while talking to Margaret and Julia, I asked about Alice's death. Julia made certain to tell me two things. First, that she'd been away when Richard had left for India, thus subtly suggesting that she'd also been away when Alice had died a couple of weeks later. Second, Julia mentioned that Alice had drowned herself, leaving behind a suicide note.

"I accepted these statements at face value because Margaret did not object to them when Julia made them. It was only later that I learned that after Richard had left for India, Margaret had been ill. So she most likely had no clear recollection of when Julia had come back to the village the summer Alice died. Also, later on I considered that if Margaret had been so ill that she'd kept to her bed, she probably could not have killed Alice. But I'm getting ahead of myself.

"It took me some time to appreciate the significance of Julia's suggestion that Alice had taken her own life. But then I began to wonder the following—if Julia claimed to have been away when Alice had died, why would she suspect that Alice had committed suicide? The inquest had ruled the death accidental. Only Alice's mother and the village constable had known about the note that Alice had left behind. Julia could not have known about it. But maybe she learned about the note from Margaret, I reasoned. After all, Margaret had visited Alice's mother, and Mrs. Harlan had shown her the note and even given her the locket as a keepsake. Thus, Margaret knew of the possibility that Alice had drowned herself. That was why she did not object to Julia's suggestion and the mention of the note.

"But here is the inconsistency—that same evening, Julia revealed that, though she knew about the suicide note, she did not know about the locket. When Margaret admitted to us that the locket she'd been wearing for twenty years had been a gift to Alice from Richard, I saw Julia's reaction. Julia was genuinely surprised by the revelation. Why? Why did she not know about the locket's provenance?

"If Julia had learned about the suicide theory from either Alice's mother or Margaret, she would have known about both the note and the locket. Those were the elements the theory was based on. The two went together. So, why did not Julia know about the locket? I believe it's because neither Alice's mother nor Margaret told Julia about the suicide theory.

"But let's look at the locket more closely, metaphorically speaking. Julia had been away from the village when Richard had left. She did not know that Richard had given Alice a locket as something of an engagement ring, a promise to return. The locket was not mentioned at the inquest. So, Julia did not know that Alice had ever had a locket. When Margaret began wearing it at some point after Alice's death, Julia never connected it to Alice. And judging by Julia's reaction the night of the dinner, Margaret never told her the locket's true provenance. So if Julia did not know about Alice's locket, then how did she know about Alice's note?"

"Yes, that is a pivotal question," Wilford said.

"She must have seen the note somewhere," I said.

"But where?" Wilford asked, playing along.

"The only place she could have seen it was on the shore, by the lake, when Alice was writing it," I said.

"But wasn't Julia Yardley away at the time?" Wilford asked.

I smiled. "She was clever in the way she worded things. She only ever said that she'd been away when Richard had left. She made no claims about being away when Alice had died. She was silent on that point."

"But if Julia Yardley was by the lake with Alice on that fateful day, why did she not see Alice wearing her locket?" Wilford asked.

"Because Alice had taken it off prior to beginning to write her letter. Alice's mother said that the locket had been inside a pocket of a leather writing case Alice had been using by the lake. Even the constable who'd brought the case back to Mrs. Harlan had not noticed that the locket was in a pocket. Mrs. Harlan only discovered it later."

Wilford nodded. "So when Julia came upon Alice, writing her letter, she had no necklace on."

I nodded. "Yes. Something transpired between the two women on the shore. An argument, most likely. Maybe Julia hit Alice accidentally; maybe it was more intentional. The result was that Alice sustained a bruise on the head and drowned. Now, Julia had to decide what to do with Alice's letter. She could dispose of it. But she no doubt read it and discovered that it was a farewell letter that worked quite well as a suicide note. So she left it to be found with the body. And here is the crucial point: since Julia had no knowledge of the locket or its existence, she would not have bothered to look for it. And the locket stayed inside the leather case pocket, unseen by her. And that was how Julia knew about the note, but not the locket.

"I realized at one point that only the killer would be keen to suggest to me that Alice had died by suicide, because it had been the killer who had left behind the letter to make it appear so in the first place."

Wilford nodded in assent.

"To Alice's mother the note and the locket placed in a pocket looked like the actions of someone about to drown themselves," I continued, "but when I read the note, it sounded to me as though Alice was in the process of breaking off her understanding with Richard. So here, two questions troubled me. What caused Alice to break off her engagement so soon after Richard's departure? And why had Alice's mother, and even

Margaret, accepted her suicide as fact? There had to have been something in Alice's behavior leading up to her death to suggest that she was very unhappy. Unhappy enough to take her life. What had upset her? Which connects back to the question of why she had wanted to break off her understanding with Richard."

"Something had transpired in the two weeks since Richard's departure," Wilford said.

I nodded. "Yes, I believe Alice learned something that upset her enough to want to forsake her promise to Richard. When I spoke to Margaret about the summer of Alice's death, she described it as a happy time, despite what came after. I got the impression that it was a time filled with love. Margaret also suggested that Alice had taken a lover. Certainly, as Dr. Perkins told me, there were many young men in love with Alice. This put me in mind of a deadly love triangle. Any of the young men of her acquaintance could have been Alice's lover—Bernard, Eliot, Dr. Perkins. Eliot Yardley had always competed with Richard. He wanted what Richard had. Or it could have been Bernard Yardley. He left on a mission soon after Alice's death. This could be interpreted as the actions of a guilty man, or at least one who'd been disappointed in love. I even considered that the late Lord Tatham could have been Alice's mysterious lover."

Wilford smirked.

"So, for a while I considered that this lover had killed Alice in a fit of jealousy. But this didn't make sense. Alice was breaking off her engagement to Richard. From what Margaret told me, Alice was ready to turn her affections to another man. Why would this man kill her?

"We have to go back to Alice's state of mind. She'd been upset about something. We'll never know about what exactly, but we can form theories based on the evidence we have. Alice's mother told me that she suspected a young woman in the village had been with child the summer Alice had died. Rue was stolen from her stock of herbs. The pregnant woman had not been Alice, as such information would have been in the coroner's medical notes. So who had it been? I considered Margaret and Julia. Margaret had been ill after Richard had left. Was that because she'd taken rue to make herself regular?"

I glanced at Wilford. If he felt any embarrassment over the subject, he did not betray it.

"No. I believe Margaret had simply been heartbroken," I continued. "She was in love with Richard. That is why she wore a locket with his image. I doubt the love was reciprocated." I didn't want to say it out loud, but I doubted Richard would have seduced Margaret, not when they'd been two much prettier women in his circle of friends. And subsequent events didn't support the theory that Margaret had had a love affair with Richard.

"But what if it was Julia who had been with child?" I offered. "Once I'd considered that, things began to fall into place. Margaret had told me that Julia had gone away one summer, pudgy, tomboyish, with short dresses that exposed her scraped knees, and had come back pretty. And Julia herself had told me that she'd been away at least for part of the summer Alice had died. I'd conflated these statements to mean that Julia had gone away ugly, and with child, and come back pretty. But we know that during the summer in question, Julia was away only for a few weeks, not enough time to undergo such a profound transformation.

"No, by the summer of Alice's death, Julia was about seventeen. She had been out of short dresses for a while. She was a young, pretty woman. Though she's rather overbearing now, when young, Julia perhaps rivaled Alice in beauty.

"Subsequent events and actions are best explained if two things were true that summer: that Eliot was Alice's secret lover, and that Julia was carrying Richard's child. I don't know how Alice found out about it. Perhaps she'd seen Julia taking rue from her mother's stock. Julia admitted to having stolen from Mrs. Harlan in the past. At tea yesterday, she said that this time she had made sure the woman wouldn't notice anything was missing. Perhaps Julia boasted to Alice about her own secret relationship with Richard, to make the beautiful Alice upset or jealous, or to torment her that Richard found her, Julia, just as attractive. Perhaps Julia even admitted to Alice that she was carrying Richard's child.

"However it happened, I believe Alice had discovered Richard's seduction of Julia. That's the kind of revelation that makes a young woman break off her engagement. And it would also explain why Alice had been so upset that even her mother had assumed she'd taken her own life.

"Unless Julia speaks about it, however, we'll never know the true reason she killed Alice. At the lake, perhaps Julia and Alice argued over Eliot. The situation Julia found herself in would have made her desperate for Eliot to marry her, not Alice."

"Mrs. Eliot Yardley and her husband have two sons," Wilford said. "The younger one is at University; the elder son was only recently called to the Bar."

Then, I considered, it's quite possible that the elder boy is Richard's son. Perhaps the rue herb did not work. Perhaps Julia never ingested it. Perhaps Julia killed Alice to eliminate her as a rival for Eliot's affections, and to guarantee that, once she told him she was pregnant, he would marry her.

"The matter of Alice's death had not been discussed in this village for over twenty years," I continued. "So, imagine Julia's shock to have the Major back and asking questions about it.

Especially now, when she was hoping to be appointed a magistrate. I wonder what transpired between Julia and the Major? Maybe he became suspicious of her. He'd learned from Alice's mother that her daughter had been upset enough to take her own life. He'd seen the letter in which Alice writes that she's breaking off her engagement and mentions a vicious rumor making her life unbearable. It would not be difficult for the Major to deduce what that rumor might have been, since he'd been the one to seduce Julia." I wondered for a moment if that had not been the real reason he'd left for India, to escape a scandal. "Maybe he confronted Julia over his suspicions," I continued. "Or maybe it was Julia who got angry with him. He'd only ever cared for Alice, even though it was she, Julia, who'd carried his child."

My thoughts drifted to the woman Mr. Graves had seen arguing with the Major. Had she been Julia? Maybe she'd seen him and had mistaken him for Uncle Albert. Perhaps that was why she had wanted to poison Uncle.

Thinking of Mr. Graves made me smile a bit. Uncle had invited him to visit again in a few months' time. Much to the maids' chagrin. And perhaps Wilford's. Though in his case, I believe he rather enjoyed the challenge of catching Mr. Graves red-handed in some misdeed, as it were. I suppose, everyone needs a hobby.

"Why do you think Julia Yardley didn't steal

poison from Mrs. Harlan's stock when she was looking for a poison to use on Major Yardley?" Wilford asked.

"Not to raise any suspicion, I suppose. The greenhouse break-in could easily be blamed on the village children. Maybe she would have resorted to using something from Mrs. Harlan's stock, as she did in the end, but the rosary pea presented itself so conveniently. And she was quite skilled with a peashooter, as her husband told us at dinner that first night. So she chose a rare poison, little known in England, hoping no one would guess the true cause of the Major's death."

"But of course, in Lord Tatham's family, everyone knows about poisons," Wilford said and smiled.

"There is one thing I don't understand," I added. "Why did Julia Yardley kill the Major at all? Why did she take the risk? The Major could not prove anything. There was absolutely no proof that she'd killed Alice."

"You have perhaps lived in London for too long, my lady," Wilford said. "Gossip and suspicions are enough to destroy one's reputation in the country. In the country, a reputation must be protected at all costs. Especially if one hopes to be a magistrate."

We turned to watch a Rolls Royce Phantom as it began its stately progression up the drive. Wilford and I had been expecting it. It was Mother, who'd arrived to collect us in person and deliver us back home in time for the wedding.

Uncle trudged solemnly towards the car. He glanced longingly at the head gardener standing to the side. The man had a sturdy arm around the pot containing Uncle's rosary pea. The scene put one in mind of a French nobleman ascending the scaffold on his way to the guillotine, giving a final farewell nod to his children left in the care of a governess whose fondness for her charges was dubious at best.

Uncle had been forced to miss the Worcestershire Flower Show today, on account of the police inquiry. To add insult to injury, he'd received a telegram just minutes ago that Lord Fetherly had collected the blue ribbon for a most poisonous plant with his giant hogweed entry. Uncle kicked at a few gravel stones with the tip of his shoe before getting into Mother's car.

"We followed the progress of your investigation in the cards," Aunt Mavis exclaimed the moment Uncle and I stepped through the doors of the family pile.

I smiled. "Oh, yes?" I asked, humoring her.

"How you failed to see that woman—" began Aunt Mavis.

"Tall. Blonde. Too sure of herself," put in Aunt

Mable.

"The Empress card kept coming up," Aunt Myrtle elucidated.

"—adding poison to Bertie's tea at the Vicarage, is beyond us," concluded Aunt Mavis.

"Why did you not warn me?!" I cried.

"We tried communicating with you," said Aunt Mavis reproachfully, "but you kept your third eye closed the entire time you were at Bertie's."

It would never have occurred to them to send a telegram instead.

The End

Thank you for reading *A Cup Full of Poison*, Book 10 of the Lady Caroline Murder Mysteries. Lady Caroline's adventures continue in the next book in the series.
Press **"Follow"** under my Amazon profile to get notified when the next book is published.

If you are a seasoned reader of the Lady Caroline series, you know that I research my books extensively. I share the best bits of research for each book in posts called **Historical Notes** on my website.
To read the Historical Notes for this book, discussing everything from rosary pea

seeds to letter writing cases, visit the historical notes section on my website: https://isabellabassett.com/category/historical-notes/

On my website you can also learn more about the Lady Caroline series, sign up for my emails, get in touch with me, learn about the other mystery series I write, or to read about beautiful Switzerland, where I live: https://isabellabassett.com

If this is your first Lady Caroline book, Lady Caroline's adventures as Uncle Albert's secretary begin in:
Murder at the Grand Hotel

BOOKS BY ISABELLA BASSETT

The Lady Caroline Murder Mysteries, a 1920s historical mysteries series about a London 'it' girl compelled to be her batty uncle's secretary.

Book 1: Murder at the Grand Hotel
Book 2: Death in the Garden
Book 3: A Body in the Villa
Book 4: Trouble on a Country Lane
Book 5: Secret of the Scarab
Book 6: A Murder Before Christmas
Book 7: A Matter of Dead Ends
Book 8: Peril in the Alps
Book 9: A Case by the Seaside

The Old Bookstore Mysteries series about an old Swiss bookstore with a peculiar black cat.

Book 1: Out of Print
Book 2: Murderous Misprint
Book 3: Suspicious Small Print

Book 4: Reckless Reprint
Book 5: Incriminating Imprint
Book 6: Scandalous Snow Print
Book 7: Blackmail Blueprint

Printed in Dunstable, United Kingdom